FINDING SILENCE

FREYA BARKER

FINDING SILENCE

Copyright © 2024 Freya Barker

All rights reserved.

No part of this publication may be reproduced, distributed, or transmitted in any form or by any means, including photocopying, recording, or by other electronic or mechanical methods, without the prior written permission of the author or publisher, except in the case of brief quotations embodied in used critical reviews and certain other non-commercial uses as permitted by copyright law. For permission requests, write to the author, mentioning in the subject line: "Reproduction Request" at the following address:

freyabarker.writes@gmail.com

This book is a work of fiction and any resemblance to any place, person or persons, living or dead, any event, occurrence, or incident is purely coincidental. The characters, places, and story lines are created and thought up from the author's imagination or are used fictitiously.

9781998529162

Cover Design: Freya Barker
Editing: Karen Hrdlicka
Proofing: Joanne Thompson

FREYA BARKER

Phyllis (Phil) Dubois has long left her performing days behind, opting for a more anonymous role in the music industry instead. Something not everyone is happy about.

When the pressure for her to return to the stage mounts, she packs her things in an old RV and hits the road in search of some peace and quiet.

She thinks she's found it when she rolls into the small town of Silence.

Former sheriff, Brant Colter, is still trying to get used to his abrupt retirement after a health scare last year. He's not good with change and likes things just the way they are.

That's why, when a purple-haired hippie moves into the empty house down the road, he's convinced trouble won't be too far behind.

He's not wrong. However, it's not his annoyingly cheerful neighbor he should be worried about, but the danger that follows her to town.

CHAPTER 1

P*hil*

"This is the one."

I've never been more sure of anything in my life.

If Mom were still kicking around, she'd be giving me a hard time for being so impulsive. She might have had a point, given I rolled into town less than four hours ago, and am about to put an offer in on a house.

What can I say? Who wouldn't fall in love on the spot with this beautiful town nestled between stunning mountains? Hell, I was so taken, I found the one and only realtor's office and walked right in, and am now about to buy my own little slice of this heavenly place.

"Are you sure?" Rowan, the realtor I dragged into my house-hunting mission, checks. "You haven't seen the inside of the place yet."

I spread my arms wide and twirl around in the dirt

driveway.

"It won't matter," I assure her. "If I don't like what's there, it can be changed."

"I suppose," the younger woman mutters as she flips through the file folder she's been carrying around. "At least it's had an inspection done when it was first listed four months ago, and it passed. It looks like the building is structurally sound anyway."

I turn to face her, grinning wide. "See? When it's right, you just know." I pat a hand on my chest. "In here."

Rowan smiles a little uneasily, probably not used to someone like me. Someone who has taken a vow to live in the moment; to let the heart and not the mind rule.

The house itself is cute, but not necessarily remarkable. I think it might even be one of those prefab designs with one small dormer above the porch to the front door, and one over what looks to be a garage. But I do like the contrast of the natural beams of the porch and the slate gray siding and slightly darker trim. It looks fresh.

"It's a little over twenty-five-hundred square feet, has three bedrooms—or two and an office—a loft, and two-and-a-half baths," Rowan rattles off.

"It sits on the edge of a beautiful creek with rapids, on a property awash with wildflowers, with three-hundred-and-sixty-degree views of the mountains," I add. "When I'm in the house I'll be looking out, and that's going to be my view. That's why those things are more important to me. To top it off, this place is about five minutes from the sweetest little town I've ever seen. As far as I'm concerned, this place was made for me," I gush.

"I'm getting that sense," Rowan observes dryly, cracking a grin. "Do you at least want to have a peek inside?"

"Absolutely."

When we walk in, I notice the house is completely empty, but for a thin layer of dust on everything. It feels like a clean slate; just what the doctor ordered.

"Is this brand new?" I ask Rowan.

"Technically it's not—it was built three years ago—and was lived in for only a few months," she clarifies.

"So it's been empty for that long?"

"Yeah."

"What happened?"

"It's a bit of a sad story. It was built by a local woman and her fiancé, but he died two days before the wedding in a freak workplace accident. She couldn't bear to live here by herself so she moved into town, but wasn't able to bring herself to list the property until a few months ago."

That is tragic.

"I can't even imagine, that poor woman."

When you come in the front door, you walk into an open-concept space. I'm guessing immediately to my left is the dining area, straight ahead would be the living room where the fireplace is, and to the left of that is a kitchen with a long island. The kitchen has a nice big window and a simple door leading out to the back deck, and from the large picture window in the living area you get a fantastic view of the creek and the mountains beyond.

In here it's a little smaller than my place in Portland, Oregon, but out there I have all the space in the world.

Rowan shows me the two spare bedrooms and one bathroom off a small hallway that runs behind the fireplace on the right side of the house. Off the kitchen on the left side of the house is another hallway that leads to a good-sized master suite, a powder room for guests, a laundry room, and a stairway leading to a bonus room and third bathroom above the garage. That bonus room could be my home studio.

"How far are the closest neighbors?" I ask the realtor when we step outside on the porch.

"The sheriff lives up another half mile, if you follow this road. He's your closest neighbor."

The first thing I'll be doing is putting in a good security system, but it's nice to know the law is literally right up the road.

"Let's go back to your office, I want to put an offer in."

"Right now? Don't you need to talk to a bank first?"

I turn to her, smiling. I can't blame her. She saw the old school bus I parked in front of the real estate office. Little does she know, the inside of that rambling old bus was turned into a very nice living space for when the road calls me. I purposely left the exterior alone to avoid drawing unwanted attention to the old girl. She serves as a great cover for me.

"That's all under control," I assure her.

She doesn't need to know I have what would probably be a decent down payment on the house hidden in cash in my school bus. I carry a lot of money on me because cash is anonymous, and because I want to be free to stay on the road as long as I want.

For too many years I've gone where I was told to go, and had little freedom for the things I wanted to do. I don't want to be beholden to anyone. Not anymore. I work when I want to—which I can do from anywhere—and not because I need to.

"In that case, let's go write up an offer."

I follow Rowan to her SUV.

"How fast do you think we can close?" I ask when we pull out of the driveway.

"How fast do you want to close?"

"Tomorrow, as far as I'm concerned."

"Are you serious?" She immediately bursts out laughing. "Never mind, of course you are."

Now it's my turn to laugh. I think I like this girl.

"Do you have a lawyer?" she asks.

"Not here in Washington, but I can have one by tomorrow."

I can feel her eyes on me.

"Okay, and what are you thinking of offering on the house?"

I glance back. "Asking price minus one dollar, out of principle."

She nods as her eyes focus back on the road.

"That'll work. We can try for a closing the end of next week, provided the seller is in agreement, and we don't run into any glitches."

That's actually not bad. It gives me a chance to set the wheels in motion back in Portland.

"Excellent. Now, where is the nearest campground?"

"Campground?"

I grin and fold my hands behind my neck, stretching the muscles in my arms a little.

"Yeah. I'm gonna need a place to stay until then."

∼

Brant

I SHOULD BE RELIEVED.

My heart has been given a clean bill of health a full year after my triple bypass surgery.

The surgery saved my life after getting hit with a massive heart attack while on the job. But, apparently, it left me with something my cardiologist tells me is PSPS, or post-sternotomy pain syndrome. Some people are left with it after they crack your chest for the heart surgery.

The pain has caused me plenty of sleepless nights, but I've been too stubborn—or maybe too scared—to see a doctor until now. When I mentioned it to my cardiologist, I was assured the pain in my chest had nothing to do with my heart, which did put my mind somewhat at ease. But now I have something else to add to the list of ways in which my fifty-three-year-old body is deciding to let me down.

Dangit.

There was a time not so long ago, I could still outrun, outlift, and outlast even most of the younger guys working for me. But those days are gone, and with it the ability for me to do my job effectively or reliably, which is why I chose to hand off the reins to my daughter, Savvy, and take an early retirement. She'll do a good job, I trained her myself, but after devoting nearly thirty-three years to the office, living and breathing my job, I feel as useless as tits on a bull.

Now I have this chronic pain condition that doesn't seem to have an easy fix, other than popping more damn pills. I swear half the crap I take is burning holes in my gut.

Speaking of guts, I should probably stop at Home Depot to pick up some more pellets for my smoker. I'm almost out and I really want to smoke that trout I pulled out of Gold Creek last night.

As I'm pulling into a parking spot, my phone rings.

"Hey, Toots. What's up?"

"Hey, Daddy. What did the doc say?"

My daughter is as subtle as a steamroller. No easing into the conversation or idle chitchat when she's got a point to get to. We've had one too many arguments about my health over the years, and that damn heart attack proved her right. I was still in the hospital recovering from the surgery when she laid a heart-to-heart on me, the weight of which I feel to this day.

Savvy had been in tears, and I haven't been able to stand seeing my daughter cry since she was twelve, got tossed barrel racing, and broke her collarbone. She'd been inconsolable and so had I. Making her cry made me feel even worse than I already felt. She'd been fuming mad though, telling me she'd already lost too many people too soon, and wasn't about to stand by and watch her last remaining parent play fast and loose with his life.

Since then, I've done my best to be more open with her instead of brushing off health concerns she might've brought up.

"Ticker's good to go."

"Good news. Did you ask her about the pain?"

I groan. She caught me wincing the other day and, in the spirit of honesty, I mentioned I had some discomfort in my chest and I'd bring it up with the cardiologist.

"Nothing to do with my heart."

"So...what is it?"

I grind my teeth; she is tenacious, which is what makes her damn good at what she does, but I'm not a fan when it's aimed at me. Reluctantly, I fill her in on what the doc told me, that it's likely something I'll simply have to contend with. I could hear the tapping of her fingers on the keyboard of her computer, and I know she's already doing research on the subject before I'm even done talking.

"Toots, do me a favor," I preemptively stop her from spouting off the results of her findings. "Give me until tomorrow to process before you start tossing out articles and studies on alternative treatment options and shit like that."

I'm met with silence, and I know she's biting her lip to keep from doing exactly that.

"Fine," she finally concedes, but she doesn't sound happy about it.

"You know what? I caught a nice trout yesterday; why don't I smoke it for dinner tomorrow night?" I can find something else to eat tonight. "It would probably go well with your broccoli salad," I add.

That has her laughing. "Is that your way of asking me to bring my broccoli salad?"

I grin. "Well, you're the one who made me eat it in the first place."

Ever since I got home from the hospital last year, Savvy's been trying to get me to eat more roughage, since I lived my whole life a meat and potatoes kinda guy. I'm trying; there aren't a lot of green things I actually get excited about, but Savvy's broccoli salad is definitely one.

"Oh, fine. I hope to be out of here by five, but I'll let you know if anything comes up."

After ending the call I head into Home Depot, get my smoking pellets, and a few other odds and ends I need to finish a project I've been working on.

I'm trying to build a secure pen for Angus, my rescue goat, who keeps escaping the pen he currently shares with the chickens. Also rescued, by the way, since Buck—our local vet and one of my poker buddies—keeps bringing over these animals for me to look after. He tells me it'll give me something useful to do, force me out of the house now I'm retired.

It forces me out of the house all right; I've been having to chase that damn goat all over the county a couple of times a week. I'm starting to see why the previous owners got rid of him, they should've called him Houdini instead of Angus. So far, I haven't found a way to keep him contained. At least not for long.

When I walk out with the large roll of galvanized fencing wire and the lumber on a cart, I realize it would've been smarter to bring the pickup. I'm gonna have to open the tailgate window on my 1996 Bronco to stick the lumber out.

"Let me give you a hand."

A pimple-faced kid in an orange apron walks up and starts lifting lumber from my cart. Do I really look that dang old already? It's on my tongue to tell him I don't need help, but the truth is, loading it *on* the cart caused that damn chest pain to flare up already.

Five minutes later I'm all set, the kid even strung a little red flag from the protruding two-by-fours, and threw me a little salute when I palmed him five bucks for the help.

This entire morning has not put me in the best of moods, which is questionable on a good day. Then there's the frustration of trying to drive in the big city, where every moron is in a hurry and thinks they're Chad Little racing for the finish line. Although, very few of the millennials crowding the roads these days would remember the NASCAR driver, let alone that he's actually from here.

My mood hasn't improved much on the rest of the way home, so when I drive up my road and pass by what should be an empty house to see an old ratty school bus parked in front, I slam on my brakes and throw open my door.

All I can see is the bottom half of what I assume to be a woman sticking out from under the bus, judging by the ankle bracelet and purple-painted toenails on her flip-flop-wearing feet. Although, I guess it might not be safe to assume anything anymore. I briefly register the jeans she's wearing are as beaten up as her bus is.

"Hey, this is private property!" I bark, clearly startling the woman who scrambles out from under her bus.

She looks like she's a leftover from the seventies, except I don't think people dyed their hair purple then. Her hair is mostly gray, a riot of untamed curls, which turns purple toward the ends, and she has an orange pair of glasses perched on the tip of her nose.

She's smiling, and for some reason that gets me even more riled up.

"This here is private property," I repeat in a growl, planting my fists on my hips.

The purple-haired woman mimics me and starts laughing.

"I know it is."

She pokes her chest with an index finger and leans forward.

"*Mine*."

CHAPTER 2

P*hil*

GOOD LORD, the veins on the man's forehead are about to pop.

Someone needs one of my green butter, white chocolate, macadamia cookies. I bet that would get him relaxed in a hurry.

"Bullshit," he barks in response to my declaration this is my property.

If not for his ornery disposition and piss-poor manners, he seems to be quite a handsome man. He reminds me a little of one of those cowboy heroes of old, with the hint of salt-and-pepper hair peeking out from under the dusty Stetson, the laugh lines carved deep into weathered skin, brass buckle on his belt to keep the well-worn jeans in place, and those steel-blue eyes matching the color of his chambray shirt.

Yeah, discarding the attitude, he'd make for a fantastic muse. I feel a soulful ballad coming on.

But first let me try to salvage what I can of this situation, because I would not be surprised if this angry man turned out to be the distant neighbor Rowan mentioned last week.

"Let me guess," I open with what I hope is a disarming smile. "You must be the sheriff of this beautiful town. Allow me to introduce myself..."

I shove a hand in his direction, but he looks at it like I'm spreading a communicable disease. Too late I notice it's covered in guck from the leaking oil pan I was checking out. It's probably a worn-out gasket, which wouldn't be the first time, but it means I'll have to find a good mechanic willing to take her on—my skills only go so far—and find myself another set of wheels right away.

I notice he's staring at me with one eyebrow raised, and I realize my mind drifted off—which it is wont to do—before I could finish telling the man who I am.

"My name is Phil Dubois, and I'm sorry if I surprised you by being here. I did, in fact, purchase this property and I just received the keys this morning."

I dig into my jeans pocket and produce the house keys, jiggling them to illustrate. But he's not looking at them, he's studying me, his eyes narrowed to slits.

"Did your parents hate you?" The comment so startles me, I almost drop the keys. "Phil?" he adds, assuming that explains his previous comment.

"Well..." I start, gathering my wits. "I can't speak for my daddy, since I haven't the foggiest idea who he might be, but I can assure you my momma loved me with every fiber of her being, which is why she named me after Grandma Phyllis."

That seems to knock the wind out of his sails, as his eyes

widen at my response. But then he presses his lips together, tips the brim of his hat as if by rote, and without another word, turns on his heel and stalks back to the classic Bronco he drove up in.

I stand beside my school bus, still trying to process what just happened, as I watch him drive off at a good clip, kicking up a cloud of dust behind him. It's not until he disappears over the next hill that I turn and head inside to wash my hands.

I'm grateful to Rowan, who made sure the water and electricity were turned on. Even though my furniture won't be here for another four days—courtesy of Grace, my business manager—I'll be able to use the bathroom and the kitchen, and will make do with what I can haul in from the bus. I'll probably just sleep in the bus in the driveway, but after months of hitting my elbows on the walls of the teensy shower in my rig, I'm looking forward to a long, leisurely bath in the freestanding soaking tub in my new bathroom. And I can't wait to prepare meals in the new kitchen, since cooking on a small three burner stove in close quarters gets old fast.

I'm not about to let a leaking gasket or a visit from a crotchety neighbor sour my day.

It's on my third run, hauling groceries and kitchen items from the bus into the house, my phone starts ringing. Thank goodness there's a cell phone tower only a few miles outside of town providing full service, because reception can be iffy in the mountains, as I've discovered.

Expecting a call from Grace, I'm unfortunately too fast in answering.

"Finally, where the fuck have you been?"

I close my eyes when I hear Dunk's voice. The person I've been trying to avoid.

"Well, hello to you too, Duncan. And how are you?"

My attempt at civility falls flat when he responds with, "What the fuck, Phil?"

I let out a deep sigh before answering.

"I've been traveling, Dunk. Exploring this beautiful country of ours."

"You've been ignoring my calls, that's what you've been doing," he accuses.

Good Lord, I am so tired of ill-tempered men. I swear it's the reason I never married one; I already spent the better part of twelve years on the road with three of them. If I think back to those first years on a tour bus that stank like a locker room for long months at a time, my skin crawls. The others used to tease me about my time of the month on the rare occasion I was in a bad mood, but those guys were temperamental all the damn time.

"Yes, I have," I admit freely. "And if I'd looked at my screen before answering, I probably would've ignored this call as well. So, consider yourself lucky."

"God, you can be a bitch," he decides to share with me.

I do a little deep breathing before I answer.

"You know, Dunk, given that you are calling me—which I presume to mean you need something, since I know you're not simply checking up on me—you may want to refrain from slinging insults. Now...what is it I can do for you?"

"Come on, Phil. Why are you being so difficult?" He tries for a conciliatory tone, which falls a little flat. "This tour would be a great opportunity. Our big comeback. The other guys are on board."

I have my doubts about that, but I'm sure Jeff and Ollie tell him that because they know damn well there is no way I'll go along with this. There's a reason *Listen Phyllis* broke up nine or so years ago and, as Duncan's phone call only underlines, nothing has changed.

When the band was still together, Jeff and Ollie were basically Switzerland, while Dunk and I were on opposite ends of a myriad of arguments. Not even arguments about the music, but mostly about the kind of shit Duncan managed to get himself into. From drugs to underaged girls and everything in between. There wasn't a line he wouldn't cross, and then expected me to rescue him on the other side.

I know over the years he hasn't changed much—Grace has kept tabs for me—and I know one of the reasons he's been so eager to get us back together, since we did that charity reunion in December last year, is because he's blown through all his money.

"As I've told you before, I have zero interest in any kind of comeback. I'm happy doing exactly what I'm doing."

"Easy for you to say, you're still rolling in it." He sounds like a petulant child.

"Because instead of blowing it all living like the rock star you no longer are, I've invested well and continued to work," I retaliate, losing my cool.

The man is infuriating, and I'm even less tolerant now than I was nine years ago.

When he snarls, "You're a selfish bitch," I've had enough.

"That's the second time in two minutes you've called me a bitch, and it will be the last. Here's what I suggest you do; lose my number, because I'm now officially blocking you."

"I will make you regret that," he threatens.

Not the first time I've heard those words, and they don't impress me.

"Try me," I dare him.

Then I end the call and block his number.

I feel marginally better.

Brant

"You forgot?"

After the encounter with that infuriating woman, the first thing I did when I got home was call my daughter. Unfortunately, I had to leave a message since she didn't answer, and waiting for her to call me back did not improve my mood, or the pain in my damn chest.

"Dad, take it down a notch," my daughter admonishes me.

She always calls me Daddy, unless she's telling me off for something, then it turns into Dad.

"In the past week alone I've been dealing with three separate burglaries, a gas station hold-up, a couple of domestic disputes—one of which turned out to be domestic battery and ended up with one of the parties in the hospital—that fire at the Pig and Whistle, which looks like it's arson, and to top it all off when I got off the phone with you earlier, I was called to the site of a hit-and-run, which left a senior citizen fighting for his life. I've had a few things on my plate, and I'm sorry, but telling you I finally sold the house did not make it on my list of priorities."

Even though we have a population just shy of three thousand with an additional eight hundred or so in surrounding areas, I remember only too well how overwhelming the job can get, and I'd been doing it for thirty plus years. Savvy has barely had a chance to get her feet wet as my replacement.

I'd just been reelected two months before I had my heart attack, and it had been the mayor who appointed my daughter as interim sheriff. I have all the faith in her, but I imagine her appointment would've ruffled the feathers of some of the older deputies on our small force.

We had nine deputies—now eight, with Savvy in her new role—and three support staff. It's a small operation with little room to spare in terms of the schedule, so when things get busy, it's the sheriff who shoulders the bulk of the workload. That's always the way it's been.

"Why didn't you call me? I would've come in and given you a hand."

"I know you would've, but I was managing on my own, and calling in Daddy would not have done me any favors here in the office," she adds in a whisper.

She's right. She's still fighting to prove to some she can do the job.

"So, you sold the house." I bring us back to the reason for the call.

"Yeah, I honestly was testing to see if there'd be any nibbles. Not a thing for a few months, and I'd almost forgotten I'd listed it when I suddenly got an offer last week, looking for a quick closing date."

I picture the old school bus and the woman who came with it, and the first thought in my mind is; I hope Savvy wasn't taken to the cleaners on this sale.

"Tell me you got fair value for it."

"Dad..." she admonishes again.

"Forgive me, but I saw the new owner today and she does not look like she has two pennies to rub together," I share. "She drives an old school bus, for crying out loud. And dresses like a bag lady. Her jeans are ripped."

She laughs at me. "Ripped jeans are in style, and I don't think she's hurting, Daddy. I'd listed the house above market and she paid what I asked minus a dollar."

"Why minus a dollar?"

"I don't know...and I wasn't about to ask. Rowan Harlow told me Phyllis Woods did not have any issues getting the money together. She overheard her on the phone making arrangements to have movers pack up the contents of her house in Portland and ship it here, which tells me she's definitely not a bag lady."

My mind caught on Savvy's mention of the woman's surname, which is not how she introduced herself to me, and that makes me suspicious. I may no longer be acting sheriff, but that doesn't mean my gut instincts are no longer working.

"I knew something was off with that woman; she told me her name was Dubois."

My daughter starts laughing at me again.

"Nothing is off with the woman, Dad. Dubois is basically French for wood or from wood, and I'm guessing she's using Dubois as an alias, a pen name."

"Pen name?"

"Yeah, she told Rowan she's a songwriter." She pauses for a moment before adding, "I hope you were nicer talking to her than you are talking about her..."

I'm not sure how to respond in a way that won't get me in more trouble, so I opt to say nothing. Unfortunately, that is enough of an answer for my daughter.

"Oh no, Dad," she says on a sigh. "Way to make a good first impression. When I head over to your place for dinner tomorrow night, I'll stop by and properly welcome her to town. Hopefully, I can undo some of the damage you've done."

Great.

Can this day get any worse?

CHAPTER 3

P*hil*

I DON'T THINK I've ever hung my laundry outside to dry.

My mom did when I was growing up, and I remember it used to smell so good. Better than any artificial additions to your load in the dryer.

Even when I was on the road, I'd find a laundromat or a campground with laundry facilities. But when your newly ordered washer and dryer won't be here for another four days and you run out of clean underwear, you go old-style. Washing by hand in the tub and hanging it to dry.

I spanned a line from the railing of the deck to a tree on the side of the yard. It's just high enough to keep my clothes off the ground and I was able to find some old-fashioned clothespins at the grocery store in town.

I'm feeling all kinds of country now, hanging my towels

and my pretty lace undies to dry in the soft breeze coming off the creek.

You really don't see anyone here. I was sitting on the deck earlier to have my coffee, and on the other side of the creek a deer stepped out of the brush for a drink. It was magical. There's no traffic noise, no sirens, no fumes; just fresh mountain air, sounds of nature, and blissful solitude.

Of course, I did meet my neighbor earlier in the week, and although not hard to look at, he isn't exactly the friendliest. Then the former owner stopped by the day after, and she was lovely. It turns out she's my neighbor's daughter, and is the current sheriff. Apparently, her father retired from the job last year. Small-town living, I tell you.

She was sweet though—Savvy, she said her name was—I'm guessing early thirties. Very pretty, which I would think isn't exactly a blessing when you're the sheriff and look to be taken seriously. It's still very much a man's world out there, especially when you get away from the bigger cities. However, her father clearly raised her to be the kind of woman she is, which has to be his one redeeming factor.

She brought a nice houseplant and a bottle of wine as a welcome to town, and gave me her number in case I needed anything.

I'm just hanging the last of my boy shorts when I hear the sound of a heavy engine. Dropping the rest of my clothespins in the basket, I rush around the side of the house to see the massive moving truck pull up on the road in front.

My stuff is here. I'm almost as excited as I was when I first bought everything. I'm especially excited to be sleeping in my own bed tonight.

I knew they were coming today, so when I came back from getting groceries, I pulled my school bus off to the side to give the truck room to back in. The two garage doors are on the side of the house and I'm hoping to use the garage as a staging area.

A burly guy hops down from the passenger side of the truck. I'm so focused on him walking toward me, I almost miss the rail-thin woman in a suit behind him until I hear her yell my name.

"Philly!"

What the hell?

"Grace?"

The smile my business manager wears is almost as big as her head.

"What on earth are you doing here?" I ask, as I watch her bump the mover out of the way so she can give me a hug.

"Are you kidding me?" she returns, holding me at arm's length. "You think I'm gonna trust these yahoos with all your worldly possessions?"

I cast an apologetic glance over her shoulder at the man patiently waiting behind her. He shrugs and doesn't seem in the least disturbed by the name-calling.

"I followed them here," she explains, pointing over her shoulder at the snazzy Mercedes SUV she drives. "Someone has to properly oversee this move. Besides," she adds, "I wanted to see what could possibly have driven you to leave behind a gorgeous house in the Southwest Hills area of Portland, and move to the freaking mountains in Bumfuck, Nowhere."

For all Grace's professional portrayal, she has the foul mouth of a dockworker.

"Not nowhere," I correct her. "Welcome to Silence, Washington."

"It's pretty," says the very patient mover. "Betcha there's some good fishin' in that crick."

"That's what I'm hoping," I tell the man with a broad smile. "Which is why I had Grace here pack up my fishing rods and waders."

The guy nods his approval with a grin that is missing a tooth or two.

"All right, enough chitchat," Grace intervenes. She knows too well how easily I can be distracted from a task at hand. "Let's get to work here; we've got a truck to unload and a house to fill."

I show Bert—the burly mover—and his partner, Darius, where to move the truck and start unloading. Then I take Grace inside for a quick walk-around, so she can see where all the big stuff goes.

"It's small. Much smaller than your house in Portland," she observes.

"Smaller, yeah, but not small. More than big enough for just me here. Besides, I only used half the rooms in my old house, it was wasteful. This fits me, and aren't the views to die for?"

We're standing in the loft area over the garage, which I hope to turn into my music room/studio. The dormer at the front of the house has a great view of the mountains we're surrounded by.

"Pretty, but it's too quiet here. All you hear is crickets."

"Guess they called it Silence for a reason. I happen to like how peaceful it is. Can you imagine the songs I could write with views like this for inspiration?"

She hums and nods, but it's clear she's not buying into it. That's okay, Grace doesn't have to love it, as long as I do.

"Hey..." I nudge her with my elbow as we head for the stairs down. "Once I'm all moved in. how'd you like to come vehicle shopping with me?"

She bulges her eyes at me.

"Why the hell did you ask me to sell your Lexus? I could've driven it up here."

"That car in the mountains? I don't think so. I'm gonna need something a little sturdier. A bit more basic."

"Yeah, sure," she answers, but is already focused on the two men lugging part of my sectional into the garage. "Don't get it dirty!" she yells at them.

I escape into the kitchen to put on the fresh pot of coffee I have a feeling we're all going to need. Filling the pot with water at the sink, I glance out the window and catch a glimpse of something white.

It's a goat, in my yard, munching on my favorite purple lace panties.

∼

Brant

I knew it.

That's it for the neighborhood.

Granted, I didn't see or hear much of her these past couple of days, but I knew that was only a matter of time. She doesn't seem the type to appreciate peace and quiet. She's altogether too colorful for that.

Driving by the house just now, it was impossible to miss the massive truck parked out front, and I happened to catch a couple of guys carrying guitars and what looked like a keyboard into her house. I'm telling you; this place is going to be party central, and I don't know if the half mile that separates us is going to be enough. Already there's a fancy-schmancy Mercedes parked on the side of the damn public road I had to swerve around.

City folk are all the same, and it's only going to get worse when that developer gets his hands on Bender's old homestead south of town. I hear they're wanting to flatten the farmhouse and build an entire resort right along the creek. So far Bender has been able to ward off the developers, but he's going into a seniors' home in Spokane where his children and grandchildren live. He'll need the money; he won't be able to hold off forever.

I put the last of my groceries away and head out to drive the pickup up to the barn so I can haul the bags of feed from the back.

Bella—the mare Marie used to ride—is munching on the long grass by the fence post when I pass by. She's old by a horse's standard at twenty-five but still enjoying her old age, and she'll have a home here for as long as she keeps her health.

An added benefit is that she keeps the young ones in check. Those would be Ginger, an American Quarter horse, and Mac, who is a Percheron cross. He's the one I favor riding, and he's a good workhorse to boot. On the rare occasion Savvy comes out with me, she takes Ginger.

I can't see those two but they're probably just over the rise on the other side of the field, near the creek.

When I get out and head to the back of the truck, the chickens are already clucking away in their pen, looking for food. But it's not until I flip the first bag over my shoulder, I notice two of the chickens coming out of the open barn doors.

What the blazes?

Dropping the bag of feed to the ground, I rush around the side where the pen is, to find part of the chicken wire ripped off the frame and bent down.

That goddamn goat.

The next ten minutes I search for Angus around the barn, in the field with the horses, down by the creek, and in the backyard of the house, where he likes to steal the few vegetables I try to grow every year. Not that I've been very successful, it was always more Marie's thing than mine, but since Buck brought over that damn goat, I think I've had maybe a handful of beans, he's eaten everything else.

Resolved I may have to hunt him down in the Bronco, I head to the front of the house to find that shiny Mercedes I saw earlier pulling into my driveway. I watch as my new neighbor climbs out of the driver's seat and disappears around the back of the SUV. A minute later she reappears, leading Angus by a rope.

"That's Angus, that's my goat," I immediately incriminate myself like an idiot.

At least she's grinning as she walks right up to me. Angus bends down and starts munching on the ridiculous pink daisies on her flip-flops.

"I know it's your goat, your daughter told me when I called her. Angus was eating my underwear off the line."

From her pocket, she pulls a scrap of purple lace.

"Just so you know, these were my favorite boy shorts. He already ate the pink, the orange, and the blue set before I got to him, in case you're wondering why he's suddenly pooping in rainbow colors. Oddly enough, he left alone my bralettes, it seems he has a penchant for panties though."

I don't know what boy shorts are, or bralettes for that matter, but I'm seriously contemplating what smoked goat would taste like.

"I'll make sure it never happens again, and I will replace whatever he...ate," I tell her stiffly, not sure what else to say, as I pluck the rope from her hand.

"Honestly, there's no need, I—"

She snaps her mouth shut when I stop her with my raised hand.

"I *will* replace them," I repeat, feeling the heat crawling up my neck. "Just tell me where you got them."

She shrugs and throws up her hands.

"Okay, if you insist. The brand is Cosabella, and I think the model is called Allure, but you may be hard-pressed to find a store that would carry them here in Silence."

She begins walking backward to the SUV as she's still talking. Still wearing that damn smile. I try to concentrate on what she's saying, but I'm too distracted by the purple scrap of lace dangling from her hand, and those bouncing purple curls around her beaming face.

Is the woman always happy?

"Last resort, you can always try their online store, it's Cosabella dot com. You do have a computer, don't you?" she tosses out as an afterthought when she already has her hand on the car door.

"Yes, I have a computer," I return, annoyed.

Never mind that it's old and only used to read my newspaper in the morning because they don't print the damn things in paper anymore.

She doesn't need to know that.

"I'm a large, by the way," she calls, before waving as she gets behind the wheel.

A vexing woman.

CHAPTER 4

P*hil*

"Okay, I'll admit, this place isn't half bad."

I grin at Grace over my coffee cup.

We're sitting outside on the back deck, taking in the scenery and listening to the flowing water in the creek. We've just had a visit of my resident deer; at least I think it was the same one, but how does one really tell? In any event, the sight of the graceful animal gingerly walking up to the water and scanning her surroundings before taking a cautious drink clearly made an impression on my manager.

"It's heaven, and you know it."

I lean back in one of the two lounge chairs we picked up in Spokane yesterday. We were able to bring those home in the back of my brand-new vehicle. Well, not exactly brand-new, the army-green Toyota 4Runner I spotted in the car lot was a 2020 model. Grace had been mortified I'd buy a second-hand, mid-range SUV, rather than one of the new luxury ones on the lot, but I'd been adamant.

I bought an average house in the mountains, way off the beaten track, why the hell would I need some shiny, ridiculously expensive vehicle in my dirt driveway? That would make no sense to me. This vehicle I can drive into Silence and no one would take a second look, which is fine and dandy with me. Besides, I'm colorful enough by myself, I don't really need my car to draw attention.

Anyway, I was able to drive the 4Runner off the lot, and seeing as its back seats fold down and allow for a pretty substantial load in the back, I figured, while we were in the city anyway, we'd do a little shopping. So, I picked up these crazy comfortable lounge chairs that go with an outdoor dining set I'm having delivered, along with a host of other things I discovered my new place needed.

Grace stayed for three days, helping me unpack the boxes and organize the house. For someone who appears as bland as the business attire she seems to wear all the time, Grace certainly has a flair for design. Something I discovered quite by accident when I was struggling redecorating my living room a few years back.

She's pretty handy with a hammer and drill as well, and by dinner last night, all my furniture was in the right place, my things were safely tucked away on shelves, in cupboards, closets, and drawers, and my pictures and artwork were all hung to their best advantage. She'd even overseen the installation of my new alarm system which, surprisingly, was done by a local company.

This is what I love about Grace, she is a true Renaissance woman, she runs my affairs like a well-oiled machine and I don't even have to look at anything. Which is just the way I like it.

"All right, I should probably grab my things and get on the road," she announces, unfolding herself from the lounger.

I get up as well. "I meant to tell you; I blocked Dunk on my phone."

"Why?"

"Because he can't take no for an answer and was getting nasty."

"The reunion tour thing?" she asks, leading the way inside.

"Of course. Has he been calling you at all?"

I can guess the answer before she gives me a reluctant, "Yeah."

"Please, don't indulge him. He's an accident waiting for a place to happen. In all the twenty-some years I've known him, he has not matured or evolved in any way. He still believes the world owes him, and likely landed himself in another pile of shit he's hoping this tour will buy him out of."

"Possibly," she contemplates. "But don't let that be the only reason you're turning this down. Your royalties aren't what they used to be, and other than money from the occasional license to use your music, or the sporadic payments from songwriting, the income is slowing down."

I've followed her into the guest room she's been using, and stand in the doorway, watching her pack the last few things in her suitcase.

"One three-month tour could put you back on the radio, it could revive your career and you'd be set for life," she advocates.

"Oh, come on, you know as well as I do, even if there wasn't another penny coming in after today, I could live comfortably off the interest on what I already have. You forget, I don't have kids to send through school or a family to sustain."

I turn my most disarming grin on her, because I don't really want to end her visit here on a sour note.

"And now I don't have an expensive lifestyle to maintain anymore either."

When she tries to pass me with her suitcase, I catch her in a big bear hug, which she endures stiffly. But as usual, she's cracked a smile by the time I let her go.

"You're lucky you have me looking after you," she grumbles when we walk out the front door.

"Yes, I am, and it's a comfort to know if ever I were to forget, you'd be right there reminding me."

She opens the back door and tosses her suitcase in, closing it again with a disgusted look on her face.

"I'm never gonna get the smell of goat out," she complains. "Thanks a lot."

"It was for a good cause, and you can charge me for the most comprehensive detailing package you can find."

She shakes her head and gets behind the wheel, gagging dramatically as she rolls down all her windows, leaning out to glare at me.

"You're a pain in my ass."

"And yet you love me like I'm blood," I tell her.

Then I jog behind her car to the end of my driveway and into the road, and—with a big smile on my face—jump up and down and wave goodbye with both my arms in the air until she disappears in a cloud of dust.

When I turn around, I catch sight of my neighbor's pickup behind me, stopped dead in the middle of the road. He's leaning over his steering wheel, squinting through the windshield at me.

Lovely.

I'm sure I didn't earn any points in the man's esteem.

BRANT

THE WOMAN IS NUTS.

Either that, or she's an alien.

Not that I believe in that kind of hogwash, but damn if she doesn't make me consider the possibility there are, in fact, little green men. Or in her case, purple-haired women.

What sane person would stand in the middle of the road doing jumping jacks? Or shove a rank goat in the back seat of a Mercedes for that matter?

Better yet, who, with full faculties intact, would pay fifty-five goddamn dollars on a scrap of lace the size of my hand? Fifty-five dollars for one single pair of those panties she likes. I buy a darn five-pack of boxers for ten bucks, and those are sturdy cotton that can last a good long time.

I'd picked up my mail yesterday afternoon on my way to the poker game. Buck's place is right by the post office. I'd noticed the white foil envelope but it didn't register until I finally got around to opening my mail this morning, this was the order I placed online a couple of days ago. I guess I wasn't expecting it so soon, but I reckon for fifty-five blasted dollars per pair of panties—and I bought four; one in every color my miserable goat ate—they'd better be delivered in two days.

A bit of a shocker though, sitting in my kitchen enjoying a cup of coffee and having those colorful bits of fabric slide onto my kitchen table. Unfortunately, there is little wrong with my imagination, and I had no trouble at all picturing

Phil—or whatever her name is—in nothing but those bright scraps of lace. The woman is built like a brick house, although I'm sure that descriptor is no longer acceptable these days.

And now she's dancing, or doing whatever she's doing, in the middle of the damn road. She's like a child in a woman's body.

I don't even have a chance to decide whether to stop and hand off the package as I'd intended, or keep on driving down the road pretending I'm on my way somewhere, which may be the safer option. She's already knocking on my window, which I reluctantly roll down.

"Morning!" she chirps, wearing that smile which seems to be a permanent fixture on her face.

Seriously. How much can one smile about in a day?

"Mornin'," I echo.

"You just caught me saying goodbye to my friend."

I guess that sort of explains the spectacle I witnessed.

"Right."

"She was helping me move in. You may have noticed the moving truck a couple of days ago? I've got all my stuff here now. Oh," she adds, blabbering on, clearly not needing any encouragement in the way of a response. "And did you see I got new wheels? I left the bus with Clem at Main Street Mechanics to get serviced. It had a leaking gasket."

"Clem's a good guy," I find myself sharing.

She grins even wider. "I hope so, he appears to be the only game in town."

"Has been since Davy Jefferson closed down his place and moved out to Coeur d'Alene."

"Why'd he leave?"

I shrug, surprised to find myself pulled into a conversation.

"Divorce, change of scenery. He's working in the service department at a Chrysler dealership now. Fewer headaches, I guess. Anyway, a lot of folks go into Spokane for service, but I prefer Clem, he's not gonna screw you over."

"Good to know. Anyway, I'm sorry I was blocking the road," she says, stepping back from the truck. "I'll let you get on your way."

She's already heading up her driveway when I suddenly stick my head out the window to call after her.

"Actually, I was coming to see you. I mean, to drop something off."

She doesn't even stop walking, just turns her head and yells back, "Great! Come on in, I've got coffee."

I have no choice but to pull into her drive and park beside the *new wheels* she mentioned. Then I grab the envelope I quickly shoved her underthings back into, and exit the truck.

She leaves the front door open and when I step up on the porch, I can see her moving around inside.

"Well, don't just stand there," she calls out. "I'm pretty easygoing, so by all means, keep the boots and hat on if you like."

I take her up on the boots—the rustic plank floor Savvy picked for the house was meant to withstand wear and tear—but my momma would roll in her grave if I didn't take off my hat indoors.

I slip it off and give it a good whack against my leg to clear the dust, and run my free hand through my hair before I step over the threshold. There are a couple of wrought iron hooks mounted on the wall above a narrow bench in the entryway, with her daisy flip-flops haphazardly kicked underneath. As I hang my hat on a hook, I peek into her living space.

The first thing I notice is the large purple leather sectional sofa, taking up most of the living area. It's like a big U, with a corner sofa and a chaise on one side. And it's purple. I didn't even know they made purple couches.

"I'm surprised you got an army-green vehicle."

She looks up from behind the kitchen island and flashes that bright smile at me.

"How so?"

"Purple appears to be your favorite color," I point out.

It makes her laugh, and right now, standing in her living room, looking at her purple couch, the sound of her laughing does funny things to my stomach.

"It absolutely is. Cream or sugar?"

"Black, please."

I notice the rest of the room is pretty sparse: a coffee table, a small side table, and a sleek low entertainment center with a fair-sized TV, a stereo, and a decent collection of CDs. Some interesting art on the walls, one big fat candle on a rustic dining set table, and little else.

"What's that?"

She's pointing at the white package I'm still clenching in my hand.

"Oh, this. It's your...uh...order from that store."

I drop it on the kitchen island and try not to look at her as she examines the content.

"You really didn't have to do this, but I want you to know I appreciate the gesture," she graciously thanks me. "Now, how about we take this coffee out back? You *have* to try out these loungers I picked up."

Next thing I know, I'm sitting back on her deck, my legs stretched out in front of me on what arguably is one of the most comfortable lounge chairs I've ever had my butt in. Not that there've been many.

"You're right, these are comfortable enough to sleep on."

"Oh, I plan to at some point."

"Just beware we have bears out here," I caution her. "They're especially active August and September, when the salmon run."

"I can't wait," she exclaims, undaunted. Then she points at a nice collection of rods I hadn't noticed leaning against the small shed near the creek's edge. "I cast a few times, but haven't had as much as a nibble yet, I was wondering if I'd picked the one creek without any fish to live next to."

I don't think this woman will ever cease to surprise me. Fishing?

"You like fishing?" Stupid question, since it's obvious. She's got some nice fly rods too.

"Love it. It's so peaceful and relaxing. It's one of the reasons I fell in love with this place. These views and a good-sized creek in the backyard, what more could you want?"

What more, indeed.

I study her for a moment, her purple hair and boldly printed shirt, but with eyes aimed at what I know to be a gorgeous view, and wearing that perpetual smile on her lips.

Who'd have thought she and I would have some things in common?

"Mayfly."

She startles and looks at me with wide eyes.

"Sorry?"

I point at her rods.

"Brook trout in the creek; they'll go for a mayfly."

CHAPTER 5

P*hil*

I'M HUFFING by the time I get back to the Toyota.

I just walked away from Silence's weekly farmer's market with two large grocery bags loaded with food. I'll never be able to eat all this stuff, but I felt compelled to buy a little something from every vendor.

My neighbor told me about the market earlier this week, when he stopped by to drop off the Cosabella underwear he insisted on buying for me. I had a hard time not laughing at his pained expression when I opened the package. I do feel a little guilty though—those panties aren't exactly cheap—but the man had been adamant he intended to replace them.

Anyway, he ended up coming in for a coffee and, although he didn't stay long, it was a good little visit. Long enough for me to learn about this market, and the fact

Silence's former sheriff isn't the A-hole he almost had me believe he was. Surprisingly, we discovered we had at least one interest in common; we both love fishing.

We chitchatted a little. Well, it was mostly me talking, since Brant doesn't say a whole lot, even when he's not being a grump. I did mention I'd met his lovely daughter but was hesitant to ask any personal questions, even though I was curious as hell.

I get the sense from the man he wouldn't appreciate prying, and I totally get that. It's not like I'm that forthcoming with information, although I did let it drop to Rowan I work in the music industry. It happened when I took her out for a celebratory dinner after the sale of the house went through, and I ended up imbibing a little too generously.

I have no illusions the information isn't going to come out at some point in time, but I would prefer for folks to have a chance to get to know the *regular* me first.

The biggest drawback of having a public career is not being allowed a private life. You become public property and people treat you differently. It's like walking around with a giant spotlight on you wherever you go, exposing even the tiniest of flaws and sometimes creating ones that aren't there. There is zero privacy, unless you create a secure bubble to live in, which I did for way too many years.

Here, in Silence, I'm able to walk into the grocery store or shop at the farmer's market. Sure, people are curious, but that's because I'm new in town. It would be the same for anyone else who moved here, but at least they're not automatically judging me. Although, I'm not so sure about that woman I bought a jar of strawberry jam from. She gave my hair a good look before I got the full body scan, and she was barely civil. She was definitely judging.

Closing the gate on my SUV after I dump my bags in the back, I happen to notice a hair salon next to the coffee shop I promised myself I'd check out after the market.

I've been waiting for the purple I dyed my hair for the charity concert to grow out, but maybe it's easier just to get the last few inches cut off. Maybe I'll pop in after I grab myself a coffee at *Strange Brew*.

The chalkboard sign out front draws my eye.

> First drink the coffee...
> Then do the things.

> Today's special - Caramel Macchiato

THAT SOUNDS RIGHT up my alley. I don't indulge often—these days my hips are eager recipients of unnecessary calories—but every now and then I crave that rich sweetness.

As I push open the door, I hear my name called. I smile when I spot Savvy in a booth at the back of the coffee shop, waving me over.

"Come join me!"

Every set of eyes in the place is now fixed on me, so I quickly walk over.

"Let me grab a coffee first. Can I get you anything?"

"I'm good, and your coffee is on me. What would you like?" Savvy counters.

I notice she has what looks like a macchiato in front of

her. The mound of whipped cream and drizzled caramel makes my mouth water.

I point at it. "One of those."

"Gotcha." Then she fixes her eyes on the woman behind the counter and calls out, "Bess, can I have another caramel macchiato for my friend Phil?"

"You betcha. One macchiato coming up," she calls back.

Savvy turns back to me, a satisfied grin on her face.

"You did that on purpose, didn't you?"

She shrugs. "Fastest way to get the nosy Parkers to stop gawking and whispering behind your back."

"*And* endorsing my character by identifying me as a friend," I add. "To the sheriff, no less."

"Probably doesn't hurt," she admits. "Although, for some it might be a strike against you. Not everyone likes me in the role of sheriff."

"I appreciate the show of support either way," I assure her.

"It's me who's grateful. Not only because you removed the albatross from around my neck and paid generously for it, but also because you appear to have breathed some life into my father's ho-hum existence."

"I have?"

I'm not aware of any such thing, but I sure am curious to know how she came to that conclusion.

"One caramel macchiato, and a couple of apple blueberry turnovers on the house," Bess announces, setting my coffee and the two pastries on the table. "You two can be my guinea pigs, it's a new recipe I'm trying out."

She slips back behind the counter before I can thank her.

"Why do you think I come in here to drink my coffee on Fridays?" Savvy shares with a grin as she grabs one of the turnovers. "Bess always does her baking for the weekend."

"Smart."

I grab my own pastry and take a bite of the flaky confection, groaning as the flavors hit my tongue. My hips are in big trouble.

"And to answer your question," Savvy says, still chewing. "Yes, you have. Dad shared about Angus's latest escapade, and how you showed up with the stupid goat and a half-chewed pair of panties. He can't get a bead on you; he's rattled."

She leans across the table.

"You do him good."

I bark out a laugh. "I seriously question whether your father would agree with you."

She sits back in her chair, smiles smugly, and shoves another bite of pastry in her mouth. I'm about to do the same when a familiar ringtone sounds from the depths of my leather tote. Of course, it takes forever to locate my damn phone on the very bottom, and by that time the ringing has stopped. I just notice the missed call was Grace when it rings again.

"I'm sorry, I have to take this."

I start getting up from the table when Savvy stops me.

"Don't get up, I've got to use the facilities anyway," she informs me as she stands up.

"Thanks."

Watching her head for the restrooms, I answer my manager's call.

"Morning, Grace. You must really miss me."

"I gather you haven't been online this morning?" she starts, giving me an uneasy feeling in the pit of my stomach.

"Haven't touched any electronics until you called. Why?"

"Good, and take my advice; don't. It's bad for your blood pressure and I'm handling it."

"If that is meant to be reassuring, I have news for you; it's *not*," I snap at her before asking, "What exactly are you handling?"

"Just some gossip rag story gone viral online overnight. I've already got your legal shark on it."

Dammit. One of the major pitfalls of fame is dealing with the press, both legit and tabloid varieties. Both are always looking to dig up a salient story to sell, but the tabloids will go so far as to create one that doesn't exist.

"How bad is it?"

"Well...it comes with pictures, but like I said, I'm on it."

Fuck me, pictures are never good.

"But I also have some good news," she quickly adds. "The realtor took some prospective buyers through the house yesterday, and you've got not one, but two offers on the table as of this morning. I'll be sending you the offers as soon as I get the files."

That didn't take long. Andreas Steger, the realtor who originally found me the house in Portland, recommended listing slightly under market value and it looks like it paid off.

"Oh, I've gotta call coming in I have to take," Grace announces. "Keep your eyes open for my email with the offers, and whatever you do, stay offline."

She should know better than to say that. It's like a red flag on a bull.

No sooner has she ended the call, when I'm already typing the band's name in my browser's search bar. A page full of social media headlines pops up, all claiming the same thing. I click on one.

Lead singer *Listen Phyllis* succumbs to lifelong addictions.

I scan the story, which claims I died from a drug overdose, and as evidence they not only have a recent picture of my house in Portland with the for sale sign on the lawn, but a blurry image of what is supposed to be my dead body.

I recognize myself in the shot, but I can't quite place it. It's not exactly a flattering picture, my mouth is hanging open and I'm spread-eagled on a couch I don't recognize, half sliding off. I'm puzzled, this is a fairly recent picture. My hair is still all purple, but I recognize the clothes I'm wearing as the outfit I bought for the charity concert. New jeans, leather bustier, silk kimono, and, despite the poor quality of the image, I can see the heavy layers of stage makeup on my face.

Suddenly it all comes back to me; the green couch in the dressing room where I zonked out—exhausted—after the concert. Only the band would've had access.

Fucking Duncan.

"Son of a bitch," I hiss.

"Everything okay?"

I look up to find Savvy sitting back down across from me. I'm sure she can see the steam coming out of my ears. I'm livid.

Unable to contain my anger, I bite off, "No, it's not," and launch into a detailed account of what that sniveling little parasite is trying to pull.

"So you're saying he's spreading a rumor you're dead because he's desperate for money? Hoping for what result?"

"Maybe to force me back into the spotlight, but I have a feeling he knows that's never going to happen. However, what this little stunt will do, for sure, is send sales soaring. Before the end of today, every radio station will be playing our music. It's the nature of the beast, the only bad publicity is no publicity."

"I guess that wouldn't be such a bad thing," she suggests cautiously.

I drop my head in my hands and groan.

"It is when it's at the expense of your name." I lift my head. "Aside from some experimentation early on in my career, I've worked hard at keeping my proverbial nose clean. No pun intended. I may not look it, but I value my reputation, and seeing it dragged through the mud is not worth the money it'll bring in."

"Couldn't you fight it? Call up the press and let them know you're still very much alive. Sue this guy for defamation?"

I shoot her a tired smile. "I could, but that would only feed the rumor mill. People will always believe where there's smoke, there's fire. Trust me, I've seen people in the industry get decimated trying to stand up for themselves. With the rise of social media and all the misinformation it shoots around the world in a matter of nanoseconds, you'll never catch up with the lies."

"So now what?"

"Now nothing. Grace—my manager—along with my lawyer will do what they can. All I can do is cut off the last of this damn purple hair, stay offline, and hope these lies don't follow me to Silence."

I can't imagine this beautiful town overrun with blood-thirsty paparazzi and tabloid reporters. So much for finding my peaceful slice of heaven.

"I hope so too," Savvy says earnestly. "But in the meantime, I'll keep my eye out for any unwanted characters showing up in town. I just hope you weren't counting on keeping your identity a secret."

I shake my head. "I wasn't necessarily going to advertise it, but had hoped to have some time to settle in before it became public knowledge."

"And you may still have that, because I would never have made the connection without you telling me. In my teenage years I was a fan, and even knowing you work in the music industry, I didn't see the resemblance."

I chuckle at that. It could mean my extravagant stage makeup did its work, or I've simply aged that much.

"I'm not sure whether to be happy or upset about that," I admit.

"I just can't believe I'm sitting across from *Listen Phyllis,*" she whispers with a big grin on her face. "I can't wait to tell Dad."

Oh shit.

CHAPTER 6

B*rant*

"All in."

My eyes narrow on Buck, who is shoving his meager pile of dollar bills into the middle of the table. Everyone else is folding, but I'm holding three kings, which could turn into a full house, depending on what card is turned up. Either way, I'm in pretty good shape so folding is not an option.

Plus, it's Buck, and he's been winning way too many pots these past few months. But he's been losing tonight, and I can't pass up on the opportunity to clean him out.

I toss some money on the pile to match his bet and ignore his dirty look.

"Gotcha, sucker," Buck goads when an eight of hearts is turned up and he slaps down a flush.

He's already reaching for the pile of bills when I calmly

lay down my full house. Buck starts cursing up a storm while Clem and Jacob bust out laughing.

"Serves you right, you greedy bastard." Jacob claps Buck on the shoulder. "You've been walking out of here with heavy pockets since April."

We're in the back room of The Kerrigan—Jacob and Stella's bar—where we play poker Thursday nights. Some nights we sit down with six, but tonight it's only the four of us. Keith Jespers, our local pharmacist, is on an Alaskan cruise with his wife, and fire chief, Randy Nichols, is recovering from hernia surgery. Poker night is a weekly affair, unless three or more of us can't make it; then we skip a week.

"I'm gonna grab another round," Clem announces. "Everyone same thing?"

I was never a heavy drinker, but I enjoyed my Thursday night bourbon. Unfortunately, heart medication and alcohol don't play well, so I've been drinking ginger ale instead. Not a big fan of sugary pops, but at least it's something different than black coffee or the water I drink the rest of the time.

"Not for me," I announce. "I've had a long day."

They all look at me questioningly.

"Well, I did. Been building a pen for that goshdang escape-artist goat you dumped on me," I grumble with an accusatory finger aimed at Buck. "That four-legged garbage disposal escaped again, but this time he ate my new neighbor's underwear off the line."

Apparently, the guys think that's funny, but it really isn't. That little stunt cost me two-hundred-and-fifty bucks, which is why I don't feel at all guilty when I catch sight of the pile of chips I took off Chuck. I think that should about cover it.

"About your neighbor..." Jacob starts, "Stella mentioned

when she dropped in to Strange Brew yesterday morning, she saw her sitting in a booth with Savvy. Nice-looking woman from what I hear."

"That's an understatement," Clem claims. "Her name is Phil and she was in the shop, dropping off her converted school bus for service. From what I've seen of her, calling her nice-looking doesn't do her justice. She dresses like a hobo and has that weird purple hair, but that woman is *fine* in capital letters." He lewdly illustrates a woman's curves with his hands.

An itch starts at the back of my neck, and I rub my hand vigorously over the spot. I'm not comfortable with this conversation.

"What kind of name is Phil for a woman?"

My eyes snap to Buck and before I realize I'm doing it; I'm jumping to my neighbor's defense.

"It's short for Phyllis." Then I turn back to Clem. "And you're one to comment on someone's attire when your idea of fashion includes a backward ball cap and a dirty oil rag tucked in your back pocket, twenty-four seven. Don't even get me going on labeling her as *fine* with whatever mime you just performed, because she is a nice woman and not an object."

I realize I may have overdone it a bit when they all stare at me slack-mouthed. I already know I'm the biggest hypocrite to walk the earth, because I was no different than these guys when I first met her.

In the uncomfortable silence that follows my ridiculous outburst, I get to my feet, ready to get out of here, but they're not letting me off that easy.

"Now I really can't fucking wait to meet this woman," Jacob announces.

"Second that," Buck pipes up. "Maybe I should drop by

and give her my card, in case she has any pets that need my services."

"I've had enough of you guys," I grumble, shoving my winnings into my pocket and heading for the door.

Behind me I hear Clem mutter, "This is going to be interesting," followed by laughter.

Bastards.

On my way out the door, I wave at Stella, who is tending bar. By the time I slide behind the wheel of my Bronco, the clock on my dashboard indicates it's only a little after nine. Still early.

Savvy answers on the second ring.

"What? No poker?"

"Yeah, but we're done. I cleaned Buck out. I'm just leaving The Kerrigan."

"That's early."

"I know," I acknowledge before steering the conversation straight at the reason for my call. "I hear you had coffee with my neighbor yesterday morning?"

Savvy's soft laugh sounds in my ear. She sounds so much like her mother.

"So that's what spurned this unexpected pleasure."

"I didn't know you were meeting for coffee now. I'm curious, so sue me."

There's a little pause before Savvy responds with a question.

"Are you driving yet?"

"Pulling out of the parking lot as we speak."

"I'm still at the office. Want to pop in here? There's something I want to run by you."

Odd, this is the first time since my surgery last year she's asking me for input. Usually, I volunteer my opinion before she asks for one.

Makes me wonder what it is she's looking for input on.

And why she can't simply tell me over the phone.

I make the mistake of aiming my Bronco for the reserved parking spot I pulled into for decades, but my daughter's department-issue SUV is parked there now. The slot beside her is empty, so I pull in there.

Deputy KC Kingma is sitting at the front desk when I walk in. He was the last deputy I hired. Only twenty-five, he's already proven himself to be a good fit for the job. He was with me on my last call thirteen months ago, and was the one who performed life-saving CPR when I collapsed in the middle of a foot pursuit. He not only saved my ass that night, but ended up making the collar two days later when he tracked down the burglary suspect we'd been chasing.

"Caught a late shift, KC?"

He looks up from the computer and flashes me one of his shy smiles.

"Evening, sir. Actually, double shift. Hugo had to rush Emily to Spokane tonight so I stayed to cover his."

I wince; Hugo Alexander's wife, Emily, has been battling cancer for the past five years, and every time a light appears at the end of the tunnel, that insidiously evil disease has found a new purchase on her body.

It's hell, watching someone you love fight so hard and still losing the battle. I should know. I've been in Hugo's shoes, watching my Marie slowly and cruelly devastated by cancer. I should give him a call in the next few days.

"Damn," I mutter. "They can't catch a break."

"I know," KC agrees. "Were you here to see Savvy? I mean, the *other* Sheriff Colter?" he corrects himself. "She's in her office."

That's one thing my daughter has changed in the office, the use of first names. I'm of a slightly different era when it was considered professional respect to address someone by their appropriate title. I'd even call Savvy "Deputy Colton" during work hours.

Initially I told her she was making a mistake—afraid she might be losing what little respect some of the department showed her—but she insisted allowing the use of first names in the privacy of the office would not have the impact I feared.

She turned out to be right; it's been a year now since she was installed as my replacement, and some of the initial naysayers in the department seem to slowly be changing their tune.

The door to Savvy's office is open, and she looks up from her laptop when I walk in.

"I actually was already considering talking to you before you called," she explains when I sit down on what still feels the wrong side of the desk.

"What did you want to talk to me about?"

"Phyllis."

"Why?" I ask, perhaps a little too sharply.

"It's easier if I show you."

She turns her laptop around and I squint my eyes at the small print. My reading glasses are at home. There are several articles open on the screen, all seem to be on the same subject.

"Are they talking about the band you used to..."

I don't finish the sentence when my eye catches on a picture of the band, *Listen Phyllis*. In particular on the only woman in the group; her hair is dyed purple. I struggle with the stupid trackpad to zoom in on her face. I ignore the heavy makeup and focus on her features, which are very familiar.

I grind my teeth against building anger. I almost feel duped.

"Why does it say she's dead? Is she pulling some kind of publicity stunt?"

"Not Phil, but one of her bandmates," Savvy clarifies.

Then she lays out for me what Phil apparently shared with her yesterday at the coffee shop, and just like that my anger gets redirected to the vultures circling my neighbor.

"I've been keeping an eye out, because Phil is worried the press may be able to track her to Silence. Frankly, so am I. But I'm not just worried about the press," she adds.

Leaning over the screen, she taps her index finger on one of the other band members in the photo. A scrawny guy, with a Fu Manchu goatee and a ponytail. He looks wasted in the picture.

"Duncan Brothers," Savvy informs me. "I'm ashamed to admit I had a major crush on him in high school. He's the one Phil says pulled this stunt. This picture was taken at a reunion concert they did last December at a charity event for Feeding America, as a result of which he's been hounding Phil to go on a reunion tour."

She slightly turns the laptop to minimize a few of the windows open on the screen, to reveal an article in Rolling Stone.

"I found this today; an interview he gave last month, promising big reunion news coming down the pipeline. There's also a short clip on TMZ where he echoes the same thing."

"He's trying to corner her into agreeing," I observe.

"Exactly. And when she wouldn't budge, he realized it would all backfire on him."

"So he makes up a story she died?"

Savvy shrugs. "He's desperate, and aside from him saving face, the stunt is giving their music new momentum in a different way."

"Except she's clearly not dead, and that's bound to come to light," I point out. "People will see it for what it was, a publicity stunt."

"Maybe, maybe not, but even if it does come out, people are likely to assume the person who was supposed to be dead would be guilty of deceit. Either way, Phil is going to be hounded over this."

I imagine so. She'll be a target for the press and the public either way.

"Does she have any idea how to get ahead of this?" I wonder out loud.

"For now, she's leaving it to her manager and her lawyer to deal with back in Portland, but I have a feeling that'll only hold off the vultures for so long."

"It may not be a bad idea to put someone on her to keep an eye out," I carefully suggest.

I don't want to overstep, I did that a few times when Savvy first took over the office and she ordered me in no uncertain terms to back off. Told me I either trusted her to do the job, or I didn't, but that it definitely was no longer mine. It stung at the time, but I respect her for it.

"Exactly, which is the reason I wanted to talk to you."

She flashes me one of those smiles I find hard to resist, and I already know I'm in trouble.

"Lloyd McCormick is recovering from back surgery, and as of tonight, Hugo is off the schedule for the foreseeable future, so I'm already short two deputies with a workload that requires double the man-hours we currently have in the budget. I'm trying to get some temporary help in, but I simply don't have a deputy I could spare." She widens her grin. "Which is where you would come in."

I glare at her, but she easily wears me down with that smile.

"You're asking me to babysit her," I bite off.

"I'm asking you to keep an eye out. Who better? You obviously have built up a rapport with her already. You bought her lingerie, for crying out loud."

"Should never have told you that," I grumble.

"Your secret is safe with me," she swears, making me instantly suspicious.

"What does Phil say about your idea?"

When the smile drops from Savvy's face and she suddenly busies herself shuffling papers around on her desk, I already know the answer.

"Let's just say she wasn't thrilled with the idea of a protective detail, which is why you would be perfect. You live next door to her already, it won't be hard to keep an eye on things, keep a finger on the pulse, so to speak. Invite her over for dinner, take her for a hike, maybe she likes horseback riding."

I narrow my eyes on her. "You want me to pretend to be her friend?"

"Why pretend?" she flings back with a wide-eyed innocence I don't buy for a second. "You already seem well on your way."

A deep sigh escapes me as I drop my head between my shoulders. I don't even know why I'm arguing this, because of course I'm going to keep an eye out on Phil. It's not like I'm going to be able to sit by and leave that woman vulnerable. Savvy knows it too, which is why she shared Phil's predicament with me.

There goes my quiet and predictable life.

CHAPTER 7

P*hil*

YOU KNOW HOW, when people tell you not to do something, the urge to do it is impossible to resist?

Well, after spending most of last night and this morning scouring all the crap about me that's gone viral, leaving me with heart palpitations and a broken coffee mug, I wish I'd heeded their caution.

Folks are vile, and I can see no matter what we do, the addiction angle is one that will linger, whether I'm dead or alive. I'm being drawn and quartered for something I'm not guilty of.

People are coming out of the woodwork—supposed friends of mine—who are saying the most outrageous things about me just to claim their own five minutes of fame. Hell, even my old neighbor in Portland was interviewed by some journalist and mentioned regular wild parties going on at my house.

In all the years I'd lived there, I'd only ever thrown one party. It was a Fourth of July party for the block—because it was my turn—and she was a guest. The only thing *wild* had been Sandra from across the street, who'd been drinking like a fish because she'd just discovered Bill, her husband, was cheating on her. Things became very heated between them, requiring some intervention.

There is even speculation about whether I have actually written the songs accredited to me.

But none of that matters; not at this point. No one is going to believe anything I say with this so-called evidence piling up, so what is the point? It's bound to bleed into this new life I've just launched in Silence. Maybe I should've moved to a private island instead.

A knock at my door has my heart jump in my throat.

Surely, they haven't found me already?

Instead of checking the peephole, I pull up the app the guy who put in my security system installed on my phone. From it, I can access the feed from all four cameras installed around the perimeter of the house.

To my relief it's not the dreaded hordes of paparazzi standing on my doorstep, but my grumpy neighbor, carrying a couple of rods and a tackle box, and with a pair of waders slung over his shoulder.

"Got coffee?" is the first thing out of his mouth when I open the door.

"Uh...I can make some."

"Good. I'll meet you out back."

With that, he turns his back and heads down the porch steps.

"What is it we're doing? Exactly?" I ask when I join him by the edge of the creek with two travel mugs of fresh coffee.

He has his tackle box spread open with a collection of flies, the likes of which I've never seen. He's already rigged one of his rods, and is working on the other one.

"I'm gonna show you how to catch these brook trout, and then we're smoking whatever we catch for dinner tonight."

"Oh, we are, are we?" I comment, surprised to find myself grinning at his overbearing announcement. "How are we gonna smoke it though? I don't have a smoker or even a grill."

That's something I've been meaning to look into. The grill I had in Portland was well-worn and wasn't worth loading up on the moving truck.

"I do," he says, solving that problem. "We can clean them and smoke them up at my place. You know how to clean a fish?"

If I were at all insecure about my abilities, I'd be good and offended by now, but I'm not, and I don't think he means to be condescending. I'm pretty sure Savvy has filled him in by now, which makes his visit a show of kindness. Despite his egregiously bigoted comments, I appreciate the gesture.

"Able, and willing to put down a five on doing it better and faster than you," I challenge him with a grin.

One of his eyebrows shoots up under the brim of his hat, and I could swear there was a small tug at the corner of his mouth. An almost smirk, now we're getting somewhere.

"You're on, but you're gonna have to catch one first."

"Wanna place a bet on who's gonna pull in the first one?" I sweeten the pot.

This time he shakes his head, bending down so his face is hidden by his damn hat.

"Let's see you rig your rod first. Grab a mayfly from my tackle box if you don't have one."

I don't hesitate and get to work, expertly affixing a new leader to my bright green fly line. Then I select a mayfly from his tackle box and tie that with a clinch knot to the end of the leader, feeling his eyes on me the whole time.

It's not until I grab my chest waders from the shed and pull them on over my clothes, I hear him wading into the creek. By the time I make my way over to a spot a little farther downstream, near a section with calmer water, he's already casting his line.

Eager to catch up, I spread my stance, brace against the strong pull of the water, and let out a length of my line to drift behind me on the current. Then bring the tip of my rod forward, back, and flick it forward again, finding my rhythm, as the line arcs through the air. Each time, I let the fly at the end of my leader skim the surface of the water, and when it lands as far as I want it, I allow the current to drift it back to me as I slowly reel in.

Darting a quick glance over my shoulder, I notice Brant is watching me. Normally, fly-fishing is a solitary pastime for me, so the unfamiliar scrutiny is making me a little self-conscious. With the sound of the water, the gentle cadence of my casting, and the clean air filling my lungs, I forget about him soon enough though. This is the peaceful life I've been craving, where nothing seems to matter but the moment you find yourself in.

I'm so immersed in this bubble of tranquility, I almost miss a little tug on my line. Reacting quickly, I set the line with a sharp jerk of my rod, feeling the tension when I slowly start reeling in. I make sure to keep the tension on the tip of my rod; the last thing I want is to lose whatever I have on my line, because it feels like a good size. I angle the tip down as I reel, then stop as I slowly bring the rod back up. Nice and even, so I don't allow any slack on the line that would give the fish room to spit out the hook.

"Ha!"

I'm unable to hold back the triumphant yell when a chunky brook trout surfaces, splashing the water as it twists and turns on my line. Carefully reeling the fish closer to me, I reach for the landing net I usually clip to my shoulder strap, only to find I left it in the shed.

Dammit.

Instead of trying to struggle with the fish while battling the tow of the current, I start backing up toward the shore, only to bump into an unmovable object.

"Here," Brant, whom I had nearly forgotten about, rumbles behind me.

~

BRANT

THE BREEZE BLOWS her hair in my face, and I notice for the first time almost all the purple is now gone.

It looks a bit shorter too, but it's hard to tell with those untamed curls. One thing I do know is it smells amazing, like fresh mountain air with a hint of citrus.

I hold on to her shoulder to steady her, and reach my other arm around her to hand her my landing net. Just then the nice trout she has on starts flopping wildly.

"You do it," she urges me, using both hands to hang on to the rod the fish is struggling against.

"Keep your tip up," I suggest, stepping around her to reach for the fish, scooping it up in my net.

When we get to the bank, I pull my pliers from my vest and with a quick twist, pull the fly from the trout's mouth.

"Nice catch."

She's grinning widely as she lifts the trout from the net, needing two hands to hold it up.

"Yeah, she's a beaut." Then she turns a pair of brown sparkling eyes on me. "And you owe me five bucks."

Her grin is infectious, and I find myself smiling back as I step to the side and point behind me to the patch of grass where I left the brook trout I pulled out of the water moments before she hooked hers.

"I think you've got that backward."

Her mouth falls open. "How'd you manage that? I didn't hear you."

"I don't think you heard anything; you were in the zone."

She squints her eyes at my fish, and then looks at the one in her hands.

"But mine is bigger," she concludes.

My laugh is gruff from lack of use, and a little rusty, but I'm getting a kick out of her competitive streak.

"We didn't bet on size though," I remind her. "We bet on speed, both for landing a fish, and cleaning them, which we still have to do, so you can still win your fiver back."

"You are *so* on," she challenges with a playful gleam in her eyes.

This woman is unlike anyone I've met before, but damned if I don't like her.

∼

SHE WINS HANDS DOWN.

So quick and certain with that thin, sharp blade of her

fillet knife, it makes me think I don't want to ever get on her wrong side.

"So?" she prompts me, her fists planted on those enticing hips.

I take in her eager face and nod. "We're square."

Her grin is triumphant and beautiful, and I quickly turn my back to finish up with my fish, and hide my smile.

Phyllis Dubois is turning out to be quite a woman.

At first, I took that prickly sensation under my skin to be annoyance, but I'm starting to think maybe that's what it feels like when you're coming alive after being in hibernation for so many years.

"Do you have a big pot?" she asks, as she washes her hands under the outside faucet I installed on the stainless steel cleaning table.

This is where I clean fish and game, maybe the occasional chicken, so having running water out here comes in handy.

"Like a stock pot," she adds.

"There's an enameled cast iron Dutch oven on the shelf above the washer and dryer in the mudroom through there."

I point at the back entrance. Wiping her hands on the seat of her pants, I watch her head for the door and step into my house.

Except for Savannah, of course, there are only a handful of people who have been inside since Marie died. Before last year, that was mainly because I was working ten, eleven, twelve-hour days. Since then, it's become clear I'm simply too ornery to socialize much, other than poker night.

But I realize I don't mind having Phil in my space.

I finish up the filets and am about to toss the remains of the fish in the bucket I'll usually empty upstream on the creek bank somewhere for the critters to snack on, when Phil stops me.

"Don't throw that out."

She comes walking up with my heavy pot and sets it on a clean corner of the stainless steel table. Then she lifts the lid.

"Everything but the entrails in here."

"What are you gonna do with it?" I want to know as I toss a fish carcass in the pot.

"Make stock. Fish stock is great for making risotto, fish stew, Thai stir-fry, soups, chowders, you name it. Can I grab some scallions from your garden?"

She points at the pitiful-looking garden Angus decimated. Apparently, he's not a big fan of onions, since those are just about the only thing left standing.

"By all means."

When she walks over and bends down, I force myself to look away. After I wash my hands at the faucet, I focus my attention on getting the smoker ready. Those filets will take at least a couple of hours to smoke.

I'm lighting the wood pellets when I feel a warm hand on my back.

"God, that smells so good already. I can't wait."

I turn to find her standing within reaching distance. She's even prettier up close when she flashes that smile at me.

"Do you mind if I simmer that pot on the stove in your kitchen?"

My eyes are fixed on her mouth as I answer her with a shake of my head. All I can think of is how her lips would taste. I don't trust myself to speak.

What the heck is happening to me?

"Hey...are you okay?" Phil asks, stroking her slim hand down my arm.

"Fine," I force from between my tight lips.

My chest feels a little restricted and I press the heel of my hand against my sternum.

"Do you need to sit down?"

"No, I don't need to sit down," I snap at her, and immediately regret it.

It's not her fault I'm feeling unbalanced.

She instantly lifts her hands, palms out, and backs away.

"Okay, maybe this wasn't such a good idea," she mutters as she turns her back and starts walking toward the edge of the deck where we left the fishing gear.

Before I realize what I'm doing, one of my hands shoots out and catches her wrist. Pulling her around, I lift my other hand to her face, sliding my fingers in her hair. Her free hand lands on my chest, and I only have a second to register surprise in her eyes before I kiss her.

Her lips are full and pliable, and I groan when she presses herself against me. It's been too long since I've held a warm, soft body in my arms. Too long since I craved getting lost in a woman with such fierceness.

"Easy," she mumbles against my mouth.

That single word is like a bucket of ice water.

I immediately release her and create some distance between us. What am I doing? Mauling a woman I barely even know?

This isn't like me, I'm the least impulsive person I know.

"I apologize..." I start, "I was out of—"

She cuts me off by waving her index finger in my face.

"Don't you dare apologize for that kiss. It's the best kiss I've had in years. You're a surprise, Brant Colter, and I have a feeling things could get quite explosive between us."

She replaces the finger in my face with a hand on my chest, and a gentle smile on her face.

"But I'm at an age where I've learned things are much better when savored instead of devoured."

I cover her hand with mine and read nothing but sincerity in her eyes. What she says makes sense. I still have no clue what *I'm* doing, but she seems to have a decent grasp, so following her lead is probably the best course to go.

"Point taken."

Lifting her hand to my mouth, I chastely kiss her knuckles before releasing her.

"Besides," she adds with a cheeky grin over her shoulder. "If we're going to get physical, I'd rather not be reeking of fish."

CHAPTER 8

P*hil*

YESTERDAY around this time I was fit to be tied.

This morning I find myself floating on a Zen cloud. Utterly chill, like the world could be lit on fire and I'd still be blissed out in my little bubble.

Yesterday turned out to be a fantastic day, and Brant Colter turned out to be the best surprise ever. Who'd have thought that taciturn and grumpy neighbor could be packing such heat?

First of all, fishing was the bomb. I had an awesome time. The banter, the friendly competition, the weather, it had all been great already. But then came that kiss, completely pulling the rug out from under me. Not even in my fantasies could I have predicted the intensity with which he kissed me, the possessiveness in the way he held me against him.

Brant Colter may want the world to think he's a good ol'boy, laid back and unflappable, but that man is hiding a deep well of passion I only sampled a little dip from yesterday.

After that first kiss, we talked. As is becoming the norm, me more than him, but both of us made a concerted effort to open up about our lives while we cooked and ate our spoils of the day.

For instance, I've learned that Brant's wife—Savvy's mother—died of cancer about ten years ago, and he retired last year after a massive heart attack and bypass surgery at his daughter's behest. I know he grew up here in Silence and—save for his college years—lived here all his life.

So different from my life experience, which included so much traveling and moving from one place to the next. His friends are all here in Silence, still enriching his life, while I made friends all over the world, but have barely maintained contact with any of them.

At face value it might look like we aren't compatible at all, but yesterday proved that to be a misinterpretation. Don't get me wrong, the way I was, even right after the band broke up, would not have felt so much of a connection with him, but now he seems to fit me just right.

The food was great, so was the company, and that second kiss—when he dropped me off on my doorstep last night—promised more of that goodness in my future.

So yes, today, I'm floating.

A message pings on my phone.

> Realtor called–you haven't responded to latest offer. Pls chk email.

. . .

SHIT.

I haven't looked at my laptop since Brant showed up on my doorstep. Reluctantly I take my coffee and sit down at the kitchen table where I left it, and flip it open. I immediately exit the browser I'd left open yesterday. I don't want anything to sour my mood, it's not like I can do anything about it anyway. Instead, I click on my inbox and look for the email from my real estate agent in Portland.

It looks like this one is even better than the previous two; they're offering a fair chunk of money over list price, and I notice they're asking for a closing date only two weeks out. Preferring to have the sale of my house done and over with as soon as possible, with everything else going on, I sign on the dotted line with my legal name, Phyllis Woods. Then I immediately send it back to the realtor.

Then I call Grace.

"It's done. I accepted the offer."

"Oh good. With the closing date they asked for?"

"Yes. It's empty, right? What's the use waiting?"

I hear Grace snort on the other end.

"You really are in a hurry, aren't you?"

"With this latest stunt? Yeah, I'm done. The sooner I can sever ties with my old life, the better."

I'm met with silence.

"Grace?"

"I hope that doesn't mean me," she finally says.

"Of course not. I'm always going to need you. How often do I have to tell you you're indispensable? What you do for me is what allows me to disappear from the stage altogether. I need someone out there to handle my affairs, why would I want anyone other than you?"

"Good to know."

I roll my eyes; thankful she can't see me. This isn't the first time I've had to reassure her when she suddenly seems insecure of her place in my life.

"What is happening with the overdose story?" I ask, changing the subject. "Do we have a strategy yet on how we're gonna handle it?"

"Gemma and Ken are hashing out a statement to be sent to major news outlets, and I'll be posting it to your social media accounts as well," she explains.

Gemma Diorio is my publicist and Ken Winfield, my lawyer. They're the ones who worry about public perception and legalities; who tell me what I can and cannot say or do. They keep me in check and therefore aren't always my favorite people, but I don't pay them to be my friends.

"It's basically going to say you are alive and well," Grace continues. "But these days preferring a quieter life out of the spotlight. It's also going to mention you have no idea at all how that story reporting your death came about, but that it is pure fabrication and your team is trying to find out where it originated from. The general consensus is basically laugh it off, keeping the response light with a touch of humor, because if we sound too serious or angry, it'll only come across as defensive and give the story more credence."

"Ugh," I groan.

As much as I don't like the plan because I really want to rant and rave against the lies, I know the strategy they suggest is the right one.

"I know, I know," Grace placates me. "But we have to be smart and measured about the way we respond."

"And when is this going to go out?"

"Gemma is pushing hard to get it out there before the evening news."

"Well, I hope that'll be the end of it."

"Actually..." she drawls the word, which never bodes well.

I groan louder.

"What?"

"There's one little thing you need to take care of, I've been fielding phone calls from the guys since this thing went viral, wanting to know what the hell is going on."

"Jeff and Ollie?"

"And Dunk," she adds.

A harsh, bitter laugh escapes me. "Are you kidding me? Duncan is the one who caused this fucking mess."

"Ken says you need to be careful slinging accusations. Even just to the other guys. You don't want to get hit with a slander suit."

"Ha! Me? It's *my* reputation that was dragged through the mud with this stunt."

"Right, but there's no evidence to show that was Dunk's doing. Yet," she quickly adds. "Ken is investigating it and doesn't want you to say or do anything that could compromise that."

"Fine. So what do I have to do?"

"Call the band. Let them know you are fine and this was some bullshit story. You can even reiterate you have no interest in returning to the stage, but whatever you do, don't point fingers."

"So, call Jeff and Ollie," I confirm.

"And Duncan," Grace adds.

Dammit, there goes my Zen cloud.

∽

BRANT

. . .

She does not look happy when I show up on her doorstep for the second time in as many days.

This time my plan was to take her for a horseback ride. We'd briefly talked about her wanting to try it last night, but perhaps in the light of day she feels differently. I don't think the scowl on her face is necessarily meant for me, at least that's not the impression I got from her last night when she was as enthusiastic a participant as I was in the goodnight kiss we shared.

"Not a good time?" I check, keeping a safe distance on the porch for the moment.

She looks like she's about to slam the door she is still holding on to shut, but then—like a balloon losing its air all at once—she deflates, her shoulders slumping and her hands dropping down by her sides. Even the tension in her features seems to melt off her face, replaced with a tired smile.

"Nothing to do with you," she indicates as she steps aside. "Please, come in."

"Would you like a coffee?"

"I probably shouldn't. I already had the two cups my cardiologist likes to limit me to."

"Can I get you something else?" she asks, clearly restless as she flutters around her kitchen.

"Glass of water, maybe?"

I'm not really thirsty but she seems to need something to do.

"Did something happen?"

For a moment, I don't think she's going to answer as she fills a glass from the dispenser in the door of her fridge. But once she slides it in front of me, she gives me her full attention.

"Yes. I was given the most unpleasant task of having to call my former band members to assure them I am still quite alive and well."

I must be showing my slight puzzlement on my face, because she quickly adds, "Including Duncan, who is the one who I'm positive initiated that story in the first place."

Right, the guitarist first Savvy, and then Phil herself, told me about.

"Why would you call him?"

"Because my lawyer wants me to treat him like the other two. He doesn't want me to let on I think Dunk is the one to blame. Afraid I'll get slapped with a defamation suit or something. All I know is talking to him, after I blocked his ass from my life, was less pleasant than the colonoscopy I was subjected to last year." She reaches for the coffeepot and fills her mug. "At least I had the presence of mind to record the conversation this time. He was his usual charming self," she adds with obvious sarcasm.

I carefully put the glass down I'd been sipping from.

"Did you tell him you were recording?"

Her eyes snap up when she picks up on the tense note in my voice.

"Of course not, he wouldn't have shown his true colors if I had."

"Good, because it's a crime to record someone without their consent in the state of Washington. If he found out, he could make trouble for you."

"Are you serious?"

"As a heartbeat. I know Oregon is a one-party consent state when it comes to phone conversations, but here in

Washington there's a clear two-party consent rule for any type of recording."

"That son of a bitch," she snaps as she swings around and braces herself on the kitchen sink, hanging her head low. "The smug bastard as much as admitted being responsible and I was hoping at least I could use his own words against him."

From the rise and fall of her back, I'd say she is working hard to get herself under control. I'm happy to grant her that time while I give her dilemma some thought.

It says something about how taken I am with this woman; I'm actually considering ignoring the law I spent over thirty years following to the letter for *her*.

"Let me listen to it," I suggest when I see she has regained her composure.

She seems to hesitate for a moment, but then walks over to the living room where she left her phone on the table. She finds the recording, presses play, and places it in front of me on the kitchen island.

"I'm surprised," I hear a man's voice say mockingly. *"Didn't you cut me off? And yet here you are, seeking me out. I'm guessing word of your unfortunate demise has reached whatever hole you're hiding in? I told you I would get to you. You've always thought you were so far above the rest of us, it made you untouchable, but how does it feel to be proven wrong?"*

Already, red flags are waving right, left, and center as I listen to the guy talk. There is a cold menace I can hear in his derisive voice that has the hair on the back of my neck stand on end. Then Phil's voice comes in, a little shaky, but I can't tell whether from anger, frustration, or fear.

"The only reason I called was because Grace told me you'd contacted her with concern about my well-being, and she felt I should put your mind at ease. But I see she must've misinter-

preted your interest. I bet you were merely fishing for information, weren't you? It doesn't matter." She immediately brushes over her own question, as if the answer is irrelevant to her.

I'm sure it was intended to be a message to this Duncan character *he* is irrelevant to her. And if that wasn't, what she says next would've brought her point home with the painful precision of a well-aimed bullet.

"In any event, I've done my due diligence and made the required calls, so now I can go back to my peaceful existence, blissfully free of bloodsuckers and other parasites," she finishes with feigned disinterest, effectively dismissing him.

But she's not fast enough and he's able to get one last, vile word in.

"Don't think you can brush me off that easily, you sanctimonious cunt! Don't think I don't know where to find you."

There the recording abruptly ends, leaving the definite threat hanging in the air.

"He's dangerous," I tell her straight out, not mincing words. "Perhaps more so now than before your call."

I see stubborn indignation settling into her features, but cut her off before she can voice her objections.

"I realize that may not have been your intention, but it's the result nonetheless. You and he; did you always have a reactive relationship?"

She pulls her eyebrows together in a frown, maybe surprised by my question. It takes her a moment to contemplate her answer.

"I guess so. It always felt more like what I would imagine a sibling relationship would be, not that I really have any frame of reference. On a creative level we meshed, but away from the music he was mostly a pain in the ass little brother. But..." she adds with a pained look in her eyes. "It sure sounds like he didn't simply see me as a nagging older sister. I'm starting to wonder if he's always hated me."

I don't like the defeated look on her face, and I don't think the offer of a horseback riding lesson is going to do much to remove it, but I have an idea what might.

Buck called when I was about to leave here, wanting to know if I would take on another rescue. I blew him off, knowing he'd probably show up with the animal in a day or two anyway. But maybe this one isn't meant for me, but for Phil. Not only am I hoping it might put that smile back on her face, but provide her with some added security as well.

"I want you to come with me," I tell her, sliding off my stool and heading for the front door.

"Wait. Where are we going?" she calls after me, staying put in the kitchen.

"You like animals, right?"

Her face lights up, confirming what I had already been able to observe from the way she was around my animals yesterday. My question intrigues her enough she follows me to the front door, picking up her phone and her purse before stepping out on the porch.

"Lock up," I remind her, which earns me a roll of her eyes.

"Can I get a hint?" she asks, settling into the passenger seat of my pickup.

I take her hand and bring it to my lips.

"Sure," I mumble, already smiling. "It has four legs."

CHAPTER 9

P*hil*

HE'S SO SWEET, I can't stand it.

If nothing else, it's those unique blue eyes that won me over.

I'll admit, I was a bit thrown by the sheer size of the animal. I'd never heard of a Daniff which, according to Buck, Brant's friend, was the cross between a Great Dane and a mastiff.

Of course, I wanted to bring Diesel home right away, but Buck said he was still waiting for the last test results to come back and would prefer keeping him at the clinic until he was sure he was completely healthy.

So now Brant is driving me to Spokane to shop for dog necessities.

I'm excited. I haven't owned a dog since Bitty died when I was sixteen. She was the cocker spaniel I grew up with. I loved that dog and was heartbroken when we found her one morning, curled up but stiff and cold in her little bed. She was my age and had died in her sleep.

I'd thought about getting another dog at one point, but after college came the band, and it hardly seemed fair to submit an animal to my crazy schedule. It's crossed my mind a few times since the band dissolved, but I guess I've never felt settled enough to take one in.

Until now, that is.

"Thank you."

Brant darts a glance my way and the tiniest of smiles pulls at his mouth.

"For what?" He wants to know.

"The distraction, looking out for me, taking me shopping, take your pick. But most of all, Diesel," I add.

"I should be thanking you," he counters. "Buck was geared up to dump that oversized bag of bones on my doorstep, so you're doing *me* a favor."

"Don't be calling him a bag of bones," I scold him playfully. "I'll have that beautiful boy fattened up in no time."

That earns me a full smile, teeth and all, and my stomach does a little flip at the sheer beauty of it. I was never one for pink hearts and butterflies—my ballads were always of the heartbreak variety—but I swear this man has me indulge in flights of fancy with the two of us in leading roles.

I suddenly find myself wanting to know his motivations for spending time with me, before I start believing in those fantasies.

"Why are you doing all this?" I gesture between him and me. "Is it because you feel somehow responsible for me? Did Savvy ask you to keep an eye out?"

He pulls up an eyebrow but doesn't turn to look at me.

"You were there when I kissed you yesterday, yeah?" His voice is deceptively soft but there is no denying the tension simmering in his words. "Because I don't need even a single full hand to count the women I've kissed since Marie died, but more importantly, neither of them had me show up on their doorstep the next day, craving another taste."

Then with a quick flash of his eyes on me, he adds, "Does that answer your question?"

Yes. Yes, it does.

His right hand is resting on the gearshift and I slide my left one underneath, so we're palm to palm. as I slip my fingers between his. Then I keep my eyes peeled for a rest stop or a turnoff.

"Do me a favor," I ask him when I see the sign for a place called Bear Lake Regional Park. "Could you pull off there?"

"The park is closed," he points out, referring to the orange banner at the bottom of the sign stating as much.

"I know, even better."

I keep my eyes on the road and my face straight, but I sense the scrutiny of his stare. It's not until I feel the truck slow down and he turns us onto the park road, I let my smile out.

"Parking lot over there."

He's clearly seen it, and pulls into the farthest spot from the road, tucked under the trees. No one is here, but even if someone should drive up, we're fairly hidden from sight back here. The moment he turns off the engine, I flip up the center console so I have room to climb on his lap.

"What are you doing?"

"What does it look like I'm doing?" I fire back, smiling as I settle myself right over where I can feel his cock hardening.

Taking off his hat, I fling it to the passenger side, and run my fingers through his short hair. One of his hands has already found purchase on my ass, while the other curls around my neck.

"Didn't you say you were craving my taste?" I taunt him.

His response is a growl before he pulls me down to his mouth.

The kiss is hungry and feral, teeth clanging and lips bruising, but I love every second of it. It's a powerful feeling, knowing I have the ability to make a man like Brant lose control. I had a hunch we'd be explosive together, but I didn't expect this almost desperate passion.

He doesn't hold back, rocking his hips to grind his erection unapologetically up against my core, his fingers digging into my flesh while his mouth plunders.

We are so lost in each other; it takes a moment to register the sharp rap on the passenger side window. I don't get a chance to look because Brant's large hand presses my head down into his shoulder.

"Fuck," he mumbles by my ear.

It's the first time I've heard him utter an actual profanity and, despite the circumstances, it puts a smile on my lips. I think I may have cracked his hard shell beyond repair...and wouldn't that be something?

∽

Brant

I must've lost my damn mind.

The last time I made out with a girl in my truck, I was

probably in my teens, trying to get to second base without getting my ears rung. Aside from the fact I should know better and am risking physical injury at my age by engaging in any kind of physical activity in the confines of my truck, I bypassed second base and was already sliding into third with my hand shoved down her pants and my fingers digging into the lush globe of her ass cheek.

Which is how the state trooper finds me.

Jesus Murphy.

I try to retrieve my hand as discreetly as is possible, under the circumstances, as Phil giggles softly in my neck.

I fail to see anything amusing about our predicament, especially when I lower the passenger side window and recognize Trooper Maynard peering into the cab of my truck.

"Sheriff Colter. Well...color me surprised." He pushes his hat back on his head and scratches his scalp. "We've had some issues with illegal overnight camping here since the park closed and have been doing regular checks. I recognized your pickup and was frankly worried you might be in medical distress. I didn't think...."

Thankfully, he doesn't finish his sentence.

The situation is embarrassing enough as it is, and Phil isn't helping. Her muffled giggles graduate into loud snickers when I remove my hand from the back of her head. But when she tries to get off my lap, I firmly grab on to her hips, holding her in place.

I'm dealing with a raging hard-on I'd prefer not to flash around for the world to see.

The eyes she flashes at me are sparkling with humor. Then she turns that smile on Trooper Maynard.

"I'm afraid there wasn't much thinking involved, Officer," she jokes, before quickly adding, "And it was all my fault."

"Yes, ma'am, I could see how that might happen," Maynard returns with a suggestive grin I'd like to smack off his face. "But perhaps it might be more advisable to find a less public venue for...uh...certain activities."

"Yes, of course."

I groan as Phil suddenly shifts to lean over to the passenger side, holding out a hand to the trooper.

"I'm sorry, where are my manners. My name is Phyllis Woods, I'm new to town," she introduces herself as if we bumped into him at some social gathering.

Pained, I close my eyes. It's not going to take long to travel through the law enforcement grapevine I was found in my truck in a compromising position with the latest arrival to town. I estimate the story will land on my daughter's desk at the sheriff's office within the next two hours.

Wonderful.

I listen with half an ear as Maynard exchanges pleasantries with Phil before suggesting we move it along.

"Glad to see you back on your feet, so to speak, Sheriff," he adds, rapping his knuckles on the roof of my truck before he turns his back and returns to his cruiser.

I let go of Phil's hip and lean my head back, pinching the bridge of my nose with my fingers as she clambers off my lap.

"Well..." she starts talking next to me, patting my knee with her hand. "*That* may have been more excitement than even I bargained for."

I glance sideways at her, but she has her eyes out the side window, watching Maynard's cruiser drive out of the parking lot.

Then she adds, as casual as can be, "I built up an appetite too. Fancy grabbing a bite of lunch before we hit the stores?"

I shake my head and start the truck.

Looks like life will be anything but boring with Phil around, but I'm still on the fence whether I am up for the kind of excitement she brings.

∼

IT TURNS OUT, I'm definitely up for her brand of excitement when she leads me into her house much later.

This is after spending the afternoon semi-exasperated but secretly enjoying myself, as I followed her around Spokane while she shopped like a woman possessed. Also, after a surprising dinner at the Hogwash Whiskey Den where I discovered, aside from an obvious love of shopping, Phil has a taste for good whiskey as well. Something new we appear to have in common, although I don't indulge in drinking it that often anymore.

Most of the day the simmering chemistry between us has been tangible. So much so that when I pulled up to her place and she asked me in for a nightcap, I couldn't wait to get her inside.

When she abruptly stops in the hallway, her hand on the light switch, I can tell something is wrong.

"What is it?"

She appears to sniff the air.

"Do you smell that?"

I get a whiff of something unpleasant. "Skunk?"

You encounter the occasional one, usually a carcass on the road signaled by their familiar pervasive, acrid stench.

But Phil shakes her head.

"Pot," she corrects me.

She could be right.

"Do you smoke?"

"I haven't since I moved here," she shares, fear showing in her eyes.

My reaction is instinctive as I grab her arm and pull her behind me. I would feel a lot better if I had my gun on me, but unfortunately, it is in the glove compartment of my truck. I reach for the light switch and flick it on.

"Was the alarm set?" I ask quietly as I take my time scanning the space.

I can see the dining and living areas, and most of the kitchen from where I'm standing.

"Yes, I disarmed it from my phone when we drove up," she answers.

"Stay right here," I instruct her, easing my way farther into the house.

As soon as I'm convinced nobody is crouched behind the kitchen counter, I duck into the small hallway leading to the extra bedrooms on the right side of the house. I flick on lights as I go, not finding anyone or anything obvious out of order.

I'm pleased to see Phil still waiting by the front door, but she appears to have armed herself with what looks like one of those Nordic hiking poles. This time, however, when I move through the main living space to the other hallway behind the kitchen, she is right behind me.

The bedroom, walk-in closet, and bathroom are all clear, but the smell of pot is stronger here.

"Garage?" I mouth at her, pointing at the door on the other side of the hallway, and she nods in response.

"Light switch around the corner on the left," she whispers behind me.

I ease open the door and immediately reach for the switch, bathing the roomy, two-car garage in light. Phil's SUV is parked in the bay to my left, and I drop down to a knee to look underneath to make sure someone isn't hiding on the other side, but no one is there.

When I turn to go back in the house, I notice an open tool box, a hammer on top. I grab it, knowing there is only one place left where someone might be hiding. Phil is already standing at the bottom of a set of stairs leading to the bonus room over the garage. She is staring up, a look of concern on her face.

"What do you have up there?"

Her eyes briefly meet mine before they're aimed back at the loft space.

"My entire life to date."

I'm not sure what it means, but it sounds important to her.

I move ahead of her and I can tell, about halfway up the stairs, this is where the smell of pot came from, but there's something else my nose picks up on. The unpleasant scent of human waste. I'm worried about what we might find up there.

Not sure how much good it will do me if someone is up there waiting, but I'm sure glad for the weight of the hammer in my hand.

"Stay well behind me," I whisper over my shoulder.

I'm pretty confident I lost any element of surprise a while ago, but that doesn't stop me from throwing open the door and reaching around the corner to find the light switch.

Phil's sharp gasp behind me underscores the devastation in front of me.

It takes me a moment to recognize the jagged debris scattered on the floor as parts of destroyed instruments, along with broken records, picture frames, torn books, and ripped papers. They even went after the love seat and ottoman with a sharp object, the stuffing and foam spilling out on the floor.

But most disturbing are the smears of what I swear is human excrement on the walls, forming the word, "C U N T."

Whoever was here is pissed.

CHAPTER 10

P*hil*

"What? That's not mine."

An ice-cold shiver runs down my spine when one of the sheriff's deputies shows me a crack pipe on the nightstand and a plastic baggie with crystals pinched between his fingers.

"Are you sure? It was in your bedside table, along with a lighter."

"I've never seen those in my life," I confirm.

"What've you got there, Sanchuk?" Savvy asks as she walks into my bedroom.

I was asked to go through the master suite with the deputy to see if anything was missing or out of place.

"Pretty sure this is meth, and some residue in the pipe. Both were in the drawer of the nightstand. She claims they're not hers."

"They're not," I reiterate.

"Probably left by the perp," the sheriff acknowledges, and I breathe a sigh of relief at her vote of support.

But, apparently, it's not enough for the deputy.

"There's no way to know that," the older man insists.

Savvy pins him with a stern look. "Don't take my word for it, but I'm willing to bet you won't find Ms. Woods' fingerprints or DNA on those."

"She could've wiped them."

"And put them back in her own night table? Even for you that's a stretch, Sanchuk. But please, process those. Who knows, we may get lucky and find something the perp left behind."

Then she places a hand on my arm.

"Do you still need Ms. Woods for anything?"

The deputy responds with a sharp shake of the head.

"Charming," I mumble as I follow her out of the bedroom.

"Don't take it personally. It has little to do with you, and everything with me. Let's just say he's not happy having me as his boss."

"Ah."

I glance at the stairs to my music room, where I believe Brant still is with a few other deputies. Savvy seems to notice where my attention is drawn.

"Dad wanted to send in for a team from the Washington State Patrol's crime lab, but they don't generally roll out for what is at this point a break and enter, and vandalism. So he's adamant about supervising evidence collection. He wants to make sure it's done right."

Despite the unsettling situation, that comment makes me smile. I haven't known Brant long, but that sounds just like him.

"Now, Dad tells me you can access your alarm system from your phone?" she asks as we walk in to the main living area.

"Yeah, I have an app on my phone."

"Can I see it?"

"Sure."

I head to the bench in the hallway where I dropped my purse when we first walked in the door. Fishing out my phone, I access the app and show it to Savvy.

"So you can arm and disarm from here. Now, does it show a history? Can you see when it's on or not?"

"It should."

I look through my options until I find a log that shows the hour and date stamp for each time the alarm settings change. I'm shocked when I find there are no entries for today's date. Not a single one.

"How is that even possible? I *know* I armed it this morning when we left. You can ask your father; I was in the truck with him when I did it from my phone. I don't know why it doesn't show up. I disarmed it when we drove up earlier, and that doesn't show either."

"Is it possible you have to be within a certain distance for it to work?" Savvy inquires.

I shake my head. "No, I should be able to do it from wherever I have a phone signal."

"Weird. Let's suppose for some reason the signal didn't get to the alarm system, it might explain why there's no time logged. But why would the signal suddenly not be received, when obviously it did prior to today?"

"Could there be a glitch in the system? Battaglia Security installed it, I could call them and ask?" I offer, but Savvy shakes her head.

"I'll do it after. Now, your system has cameras, right? Are you able to access those on this app?"

"It's easier to see on my laptop," I suggest.

I move over to the couch and lift the foot end of the chaise, which hides a storage compartment where I keep and charge my electronics so they're out of sight. Then I rejoin Savvy at the kitchen island and sign in to my account on the laptop.

"Are you almost done with her?" Brant's voice pipes up from the doorway. His eyes scan me top to bottom. "Are you okay?"

"Yeah," I lie.

I'm mentally exhausted but feel jittery as hell.

"If you don't mind me hanging on to your laptop," Savvy directs at me. "Scanning the camera feed is going to take some time, and we still have some finishing up to do here. Why don't you go with Dad and get some rest? It's already late."

"Where am I going?"

"My place. Pack a bag," Brant grunts, which his daughter apparently finds funny.

"I'm afraid Dad's not known for his bedside manner," she shares, before assuring me, "But it comes from a good place."

If I didn't know any better, I might think she was putting in a good word for him. Not that she needs to; I'm more than happy to pack a bag and eager to breathe in some fresh air.

∾

Brant

. . .

I'M STILL WIRED when I lead Phil into my house.

It's almost midnight and by all rights I should be tired—I'm usually in bed by now—but I doubt I could sleep. First, I'll need to work out the logistics of our sleeping arrangement, which may be a challenge.

What used to be Savvy's room is now my home office and admittedly a bit of a disaster, and the former spare room has become storage space for boxes of Marie's stuff I'm keeping for our daughter. So effectively, there is one bed in the house and that is mine. I don't want to presume anything, so Phil can sleep there and I'll grab the couch or the recliner in the office.

"Make yourself comfortable," I tell her. "There's juice and iced tea in the fridge, I think there may be a couple of beers, grab whatever you like. The remote for the TV is on the table. I'm just going to run your bag upstairs."

She nods, uncharacteristically quiet, and wanders into the kitchen. I carry her bag upstairs and toss it on the chair in my bedroom. Then I quickly strip my bed, throw those sheets on the recliner in my office, and dig out the extra set and some clean towels from the linen closet. Then I remake my bed in record time and use a T-shirt I tossed on the floor yesterday to wipe the layer of dust from the nightstands and the dresser. Next, I do some damage control in the bathroom, making sure it can pass muster before I join Phil downstairs.

She's in the kitchen, standing in front of the window, looking out at the stable. I walk up behind her and put my hands on her shoulders.

"How are you doing?"

By way of response, she swings around and drops her forehead against my chest. I slide my hand under her curls and find the nape of her neck, gently massaging it when I find it tight with tension.

"I'm never gonna get that stench out of the house, I can still smell it now," she mumbles.

"Yeah, we'll get the stench out," I assure her. "And why don't you grab a quick shower? Not that you smell, but I know from experience the steam helps to clear nasty odors clinging to your nose."

She lifts her head and awards me with a little smile.

"I think I might do that."

"Left at the top of the stairs. Doors to the bedroom and bathroom are open."

Her mouth is tempting, but I resist and opt to press a kiss to her forehead instead. This is probably not the time, because once I have her taste on my lips, I already know my control will be out the window, and I doubt that's what she needs from me right now.

"Don't let me keep you up," she says as she moves to the stairs.

"You're not."

For twenty agonizing minutes, filled with mental images of Phil in my shower, I've been trying to focus on some news show on TV with limited success, but the moment I hear her coming down the stairs, my head turns on a swivel.

The first thing I notice is she's barefoot, and for some reason the sight of her purple-tipped toes on my wooden floors feels very intimate. It only takes me a fraction of a second to decide I like it.

Next, I notice she's wearing a pair of oat-colored lounge pants, they look soft, just like her oversized top of the same color. The outfit is loose on her body, but somehow is more enticing than anything I've seen her in.

Finally, I notice the bottle of Bruichladdich whiskey in her hands. I recognize the distinct shape.

"I packed this. I was saving this for a special occasion," she explains with a sheepish grin on her face. "I figured now is probably as good a time as any. Can I tempt you?"

I almost laugh out loud. For a guy who's all but sworn off alcohol, I can't believe I'm even considering a second drink today.

Can she tempt me? Hell, she doesn't even have to try.

"I'll grab us some glasses."

"Can we sit outside?" she asks. "It's a beautiful night."

"Of course. Grab that blanket." I point at the throw folded over the arm of the couch. "It may be a little chilly."

A few minutes later, when I carry the glasses outside, she's already sitting on the love seat that is part of the outdoor set Savvy got me for my retirement. I think this is only the second or third time it's been used, but I have a feeling that may change. Phil has made herself comfortable, her feet tucked under her, as she pats the seat beside her.

I grab the bottle, noticing Phil has already broken the seal, and pour us two fingers each. No ice or water to dilute the flavor, I hand her a tumbler and pick up my own, tapping her glass lightly.

"Cheers."

We each take a sip; this is the kind of whiskey to be savored, not gulped.

Immediately, Phil takes the glass from my hand and sets both of them down on the table before turning to me with a predatory smile on her face.

"Now, where were we?"

The next moment she is straddling my lap, her mouth on mine, and her sweet taste enriched by the smoky whiskey permeating my senses. It takes my hands two seconds to discover she is naked underneath her clothes, and I groan when my fingers travel down her butt crease and find her slick with want already.

"Yessss," she hisses against my lips when I dip a digit inside her.

She adjusts herself, tilting her hips back in invitation, so I add a second finger. Immediately she starts to move, riding my hand while rubbing herself on my cock. It's enough to drive me mad. My teeth nip at the column of her throat when she throws her head back, giving herself over to sensation.

"Too many clothes," I complain, trying to work my free hand underneath the oversized shirt but getting tangled in fabric.

"Yes," she sighs.

I'm not sure whether she's agreeing or still caught up in the moment, but then she abruptly climbs off my lap.

"Come," she urges me, holding out her hand. "Let's get naked where it's warm."

She's already pulling her top over her head when I follow her into the bedroom. I rush to catch up when she starts shoving down her pants, exposing that gorgeous round ass I've had a hard time keeping my hands, or my eyes, off.

I just manage to get my shirt over my head when she turns around. The shirt drops from my hand and I forget what I was doing as my eyes try to take in the beautiful woman in front of me. All that creamy-soft skin covering luscious curves my hands are eager to explore. But instead, I stare, not quite believing the situation I find myself in.

Phil takes a step toward me, reaching out with her hand and letting her fingertips trace the scars bisecting my chest.

"Is this safe? Can you—"

I grab her hand and cut her off, "Yes."

Then I slide my free arm around her and try to pull her against me, but she has different plans and starts backing me toward the bed, urging me to get on.

I scoot up and lean my back against the headboard, enjoying the view as Phil climbs up after me and straddles my thighs.

"Let me do the honors," she whispers as her hands drop down to my belt.

Her eyes stay fixed on mine, as she unzips me and wiggles my jeans and boxers far enough down my hips for my cock to spring free. She immediately curls her fingers around me, the warm pressure eliciting a deep groan from me.

"It's a thing of beauty, this cock of yours," she mutters, "and I hope to God I'll get an opportunity to get better acquainted, but for tonight I need to feel you inside."

"Sweet Jesus," escapes me when she rearranges herself and sinks down, taking me into her heat.

I reach for her hips with the intention of taking over, when she shakes her head.

"Let me take care of you."

I don't easily hand over control, but when I look at that beautiful smile—which was missing these past few hours—I hold on and let her take me for the ride of my life.

CHAPTER 11

B*rant*

I SWALLOW a groan of protest as I untangle my limbs from the warm woman in my bed.

Not a cuddler, I was surprised to wake up a few minutes ago with my body plastered to hers. I didn't think at fifty-three there'd be any *firsts* left but, apparently, I was wrong. The short time I've known Phil has been filled with surprises.

For starters, I'm not an impulsive man, but it sure didn't take me long to go from resenting my new neighbor to falling ass over teakettle for the woman. Since then, it's been a series of new experiences, the highlight being last night's events. Having Phil take charge, and yielding to her control, was by far the most unexpected. I came so damn hard it blinded me, and for a moment I thought my heart had stopped for good.

But what a way it would've been to go.

"Mmm..." she mumbles, cracking one eye open as she rolls over in bed. "What time is it?"

"Six."

I sit back down on the edge of the mattress and brush a few untamed curls from her forehead.

"That's an ungodly hour to get out of bed," she declares, scrunching up her face.

I grin down at her. "Best part of the day, when everything is just waking up. Besides, the animals need feeding. Especially the chickens or they won't leave me eggs."

She pulls the covers over her head making her, "Eggs are overrated," comment sound muffled.

"You'll have to get used to getting up early if you want to be a dog owner. Diesel will need to go out to do his business first thing in the morning."

"You don't play fair."

I tug down the covers and lean in to kiss her stubborn lips.

"Stay in bed, enjoy it while you can."

When I get up and move to the bathroom for a quick shower, she calls me back.

"Brant? We didn't use protection."

Another absolute first for me, at least since my wife died. I've been careful, but not last night.

"I know. If you're worried, I haven't been active for a while. Definitely not since my heart issues last year, and I was given a clean bill of health after."

"I wasn't worried about you," she reveals. "I thought you might be worried about me, but I'm clean as well, and I had a hysterectomy a few years ago, so pregnancy is not a possibility."

Pregnancy? Christ, that hadn't even occurred to me.

I'm someone who is normally conscientious *and* cautious, so I'm shocked I totally blanked out on that. It's not like I was impaired, unless I was drunk on Phil, because I barely had a sip of that whiskey. I guess that proves my point, it must be this woman who muddles my brain, because who in their right mind would walk away from a glass of very expensive Bruichladdich.

I close my eyes and pinch the bridge of my nose in an attempt to clear my head, before aiming a smile at the woman in my bed.

"Good to know. Get some more rest. I'll be in the stable if you can't find me downstairs when you get up."

She gives me her thumbs-up before disappearing under the covers, and I head for the shower.

Every morning I make a pot with enough coffee for my two allotted cups. Today I double it up. Then I take two instead of my usual one bagel from the freezer, pop one in the toaster and leave the other on a plate on the counter. After grabbing the cream cheese and the last jar of huckleberry jam Savvy and I made two years ago from the fridge, I take a pen and notepad from the kitchen drawer and start making today's list.

It's something I started doing last year. The first months after the surgery, and my subsequent retirement, there had been times when I felt like I was being sucked into a dark void. I felt useless and was unsure of what I could and couldn't do. When the body you've known and relied on for fifty plus years suddenly betrays you, it takes a while to build up that trust again.

At the suggestion of my cardiologist, I started writing down small tasks every day, both to build confidence in my body, and to give me a purpose. It's become a habit I stick to. Normally, I note down mundane things, like groceries to pick up or laundry to do. Sometimes people to call or visits to make.

But for the first time I'm having trouble plotting out my day. Suddenly, I'm no longer planning just for me, but find myself taking someone else into account.

The ping of the toaster has me drop my pen on the empty sheet of paper, as I turn to grab my bagel. I lather it royally with cream cheese and jam and take a big bite before pouring myself a mug of coffee. Then, tucking my phone in my pocket and carrying my bagel and coffee, I head out the back door.

I immediately notice the bottle of whiskey and one of the tumblers toppled over on the table, a puddle underneath them. The other glass, and the cork I distinctly remember putting back on the bottle are missing. It's not until I set down my plate and cup on top of the smoker and walk up to the table to right the now half-empty bottle, I catch sight of the culprit lying on the deck, wedged between the outdoor love seat and the table, and probably drunk out of his mind.

"Goddammit, Angus!"

I pull back the love seat and nudge the goat, who isn't moving.

In fact, he barely seems to be breathing. There is foam on his mouth and his tongue is hanging out.

I immediately pull my phone from my pocket and dial Buck.

∾

Phil

. . .

"I DON'T THINK it was the alcohol."

I'm sitting on the deck, stroking Angus's coat, while Buck is packing up his equipment.

The last thing I thought I'd be walking in on, when I came down to check the voices outside the window, was Brant and the vet pumping the goat's stomach on the back porch. Hell, I didn't even know you could pump a goat's stomach, but apparently vets have special kits for that.

"What do you mean?" Brant asks his friend.

"If he'd have drunk the entire bottle, it might've been lethal, but half of the contents is still in there, plus a whole puddle on the table. At best he drank whatever was left in the glasses, and maybe a bit from the bottle before he went down."

"So if it wasn't the whiskey, then what could it have been?" I'm curious to know.

"I didn't say it wasn't the whiskey," Buck clarifies, "I said I didn't think it was the alcohol."

I grimace when he points at the clear plastic bag he collected Angus's stomach contents in.

"There's only a little and it's liquid only. Plus, alcohol doesn't cause foaming at the mouth." He aims a look at Brant. "How much did you guys drink last night?"

"A sip, that's all." Brant's eyes come to me and I read concern in them. "How are you feeling?"

My hand automatically goes to my head, which has felt like it's stuffed full of wool since I first woke up. Since I didn't drink enough for a hangover, I figured it was an after-effect from the stress of last night's events at my house, and tried to ignore it. Now, I'm not so sure.

"Like I drank too much last night," I admit.

He nods. "Me too."

"You may want to give Savvy a call and put that bottle in

a safe place," Buck suggests. "Might not be a bad idea for you guys to get some bloodwork done as well. I'll leave his stomach contents here in case Savvy wants it, but I should get this guy to the clinic where I can monitor him properly."

Ten minutes later, I catch sight of Brant's daughter driving up in a sheriff's cruiser, a small red car following right behind her.

"I brought Dana," Savvy announces when she walks in with another woman.

She's probably in her thirties, with fiery red hair and a big, disarming smile as she walks right up to me.

"Hi, we haven't met yet. I'm Dana Kerrigan," she introduces herself. "I'm a nurse practitioner at the hospital."

Hospital is a big word for the single-story building on the outskirts of town. From what I understand, it only has ten beds.

"I thought we'd kill two birds with one stone, and asked Dana to take blood samples while you fill me in on what exactly happened," Savvy explains the other woman's presence. "If that's okay with you."

"By all means."

Brant's reply is a grunt. He seems to have reverted back to his grumpy self, although I recognize it as concern now. I don't blame him. I'm pretty concerned myself.

It's one thing for Duncan to break into my place and destroy the things I value most—my instruments, my gold and platinum albums, my framed Billboard charts, tour posters, and of course, my two Grammys. Even planting those drugs in my nightstand is something I could see him doing, but the thought he might actually have tried to harm me physically is beyond comprehension.

Which is why I immediately sit down at the dining table,

roll up the sleeve of my shirt, and offer Dana my arm. The sooner I find out, the better.

"Was this a new bottle? Do you know if the seal was broken?" Savvy wants to know.

"It looked unopened," Brant answers.

"That was a new bottle," I confirm.

"Where did it come from?" Savvy presses.

"I put it in my bag when I was packing it last night," I explain.

"Right, but how did it come in your possession and where was it in your house? In your liquor cabinet?"

She's referring to the wall unit holding my TV, which also serves as bookshelf and liquor storage.

"Oh, it was a housewarming gift from my manager, and I kept it in the kitchen cupboard over the fridge. That's where I keep my secret, premium stash." When Savvy looks confused, I clarify. "The liquor cabinet is for guests; the kitchen cupboard has always been for me to savor. Unless I know someone has a taste for the good stuff, like your dad, then I'm happy to share."

I notice her dart a look at her father before returning to me.

"And how many people know where you keep the good stuff?"

"Quite a few. People who've spent any time in my place in Portland would probably know."

"So friends, band members, cleaning lady."

I shrug. "I guess it's a well-known secret."

"A little poke," Dana warns, tapping a vein on the inside of my arm.

While we were talking, she had spread out a sterile pad on the table, and tied a rubber band around my upper arm. The pinch of the needle is minimal as she fills two empty vials of my blood. Then she takes a piece of gauze, pressing it down as she removes the needle.

"Keep pressure on," she instructs me as she tears off a strip of medical tape to secure the gauze.

When Brant takes my place at the table, I notice Savvy stepped out the back door and is talking on her phone.

"Should I make some fresh coffee?" I ask, wanting something to do with my hands.

"I keep the ground coffee in the freezer," Brant volunteers.

For the next few minutes, I busy myself cleaning the old coffee out and putting a new pot on. I notice a bagel sitting on a plate on the counter next to the toaster, and realize that gnawing feeling in my gut might just be hunger.

"Want to split a bagel with me?" I ask Brant when he joins me in the kitchen.

"I left that out for you. Mine is still somewhere outside."

"Sitting out there for how long now?" I shake my head. "We'll split this one."

I pop it in the toaster and when I turn around, I see Savvy's joined us, keenly observing the exchange between her father and me.

"I'm curious," she starts, a mischievous glimmer in her eyes. "You bring what looks to be an expensive bottle of scotch, pour two glasses to enjoy with a fellow aficionado, and then leave the drinks unfinished and the bottle sitting outside? How come?"

There is not a doubt in my mind the woman knows exactly what her father and I were up to, and I have a feeling this inquisition is more about teasing her father than giving me a hard time. When I glance over at Brant, I see she succeeded in making him feel very uncomfortable.

"I guess the events of the day caught up with us," I

disclose by way of explanation, barely able to contain my grin.

"Are you done here?" Brant grumbles, clearly not enjoying this topic of conversation.

"I am," Dana pipes up, holding up four labeled vials. "Unless you want me to run these to the lab and get them to put a rush on it?"

"I'll take them," Savvy indicates. "Better do things by the book. Besides, I have to drop off the goat's stomach contents anyway."

When Dana is gone, Savvy collects the whiskey bottle, the plastic baggie Buck left, and the vials of blood, placing them all in paper bags she labels. Then she turns to her father and me.

"After I run these into town, I'm heading back to your place to see if we can get any fingerprints off that kitchen cupboard. I already left a message with the Portland PD earlier, trying to get them to look into the whereabouts of Duncan Brothers, but the break-in and vandalizing of a house in small-town Washington sits low on their list of priorities. However, if we can show someone laced that bottle hoping to poison you, it could become attempted murder, which holds a hell of a lot more clout."

A cold shiver runs down my spine at the mention of murder. I have a hard time believing Dunk would go there.

I know at the height of the band's popularity, I received weird fan mail, threats, and even had the occasional stalker, but most of the time I was shielded from that stuff. We were surrounded by security wherever we went, and I rarely ever looked at my own social media or emails. Grace always looked after that stuff, for all I know she still does.

What if this wasn't Dunk at all, but some disgruntled fan?

"Maybe I should give Grace a call," I mention. "She'd know if there were any recent threats or crazy fans lurking around."

"Already spoke to her earlier as well," Savvy shares with a friendly smile.

"Oh, good."

"And you likely won't be able to get a hold of her," she adds, looking at her watch. "She's on a flight into Spokane as we speak."

"Grace is?"

CHAPTER 12

P*hil*

"They're my *loony* files."

I glance at Grace over the rim of my fifth or sixth cup of coffee today. I may have to call this my last one because, I swear, I'm so charged my ears are buzzing.

My manager drove up half an hour ago with an extra suitcase which is currently sitting open on my coffee table. She's pulling out shoeboxes, file folders, and plastic bags stuffed with some disturbing shit to show the sheriff.

Savvy called after lunch and asked for me to come over to my place to do a walk-through of the house, and go over a list of the things her team is taking in as evidence. Brant dropped me off and was going to run into town to check on Angus and pick up a few things.

We'd barely finished with the walk-through when Grace

rolled up in a rental, and Brant's Bronco was right behind her.

I can feel him standing at my back as Grace pulls out one of the bags and spills the contents. Handcuffs, a whip, some leather contraption that looks like a harness of sorts, and a disturbingly large black dildo bounces off my couch and on the floor.

"What the fuck?" Brant growls over my shoulder.

Savvy's eyes widen in shock as she turns to look at her father. I guess he really doesn't swear much normally. I'm starting to think I'm a bad influence on the man.

"Oh, believe me, this isn't the worst," Grace shares as she bends over to grab the monstrous silicone dick off the floor and casually tosses it back on the couch. "Over the years, I've collected some pretty weird and worrisome stuff from your *admirers*." She emphasizes it with finger quotes. "Some of it I actually ended up handing off to law enforcement—anything that had biological material or actual physical threats—but I have pictures of everything in those file folders along with copies of the police reports."

"Biological material?" I can't stop myself from asking, even though I'm not sure I want to know.

"Trust me, you don't want to know," Grace confirms right away. "Although...I guess you had Duncan smear shit all over your wall, so you can probably use your imagination."

"We can't be sure it was him," Savvy corrects her. "At least not until we have some concrete evidence to that fact. I've had my deputies looking for Mr. Brothers but he's not answering his phone and, so far, we haven't had any luck connecting with him. He's definitely not staying anywhere in Silence. At this point, we have nothing but suspicions to go on. So, while we wait for the lab to process the evidence we've collected, I'm going to take this fan mail with me and go through it. Maybe I can flag other potential suspects."

She packs the contents of Grace's suitcase in a box Brant digs up from the garage.

"I'll carry it out for you," he offers, following his daughter out the door.

"Sooo..." Grace drawls, as soon as they're out of earshot. "You and the silver fox neighbor look pretty cozy. Any prospects there?"

I'd say there were more than prospects, but I don't know if I'm ready to share yet, so instead of an answer, I give her a shrug. Kissing and telling was never my style, and I'm not about to start now.

Besides, Grace may have been my manager for many years and probably knows me better than most, but I wouldn't exactly say we were that close. For instance, I don't really know what goes on in her life outside of her work for me. I know she's single, and has no kids of her own—similar to me—but she has mentioned her brother and her niece before.

Maybe my move here to Silence is creating a slightly different dynamic than we had back in Portland, where our routine had been pretty predictable over the past nine or ten years.

"I can't believe you never told me about the BDSM stuff," I comment instead, still processing the extent of the creepy fan stuff she brought over.

Now it's Grace's turn to shrug.

"It's part of my job to deal with the crazies so you don't have to. That was especially true at the height of your career, you needed to focus on other things, so I ran interference. If there was anything concerning, I notified your security detail, as well as law enforcement."

"Well, I'd hoped I could slip a bit further into obscurity here in Silence, so I hope the sheriff's office can get a handle on this situation with Dunk quickly, so I can get back to becoming a nonentity."

Grace looks at me, her head tilted to one side. "Are you positive Duncan is responsible for this? I find it so hard to believe he'd go to these lengths."

"Grace, you haven't heard my last few conversations with him. Or maybe those are better described as his progressively angry rants at me. He threatened he knew where to find me and called me a cunt."

I walk to the front window and peer out to see Brant and his daughter standing next to her cruiser, talking animatedly. Not wanting to be caught looking, I swing around to face Grace.

"That same word was painted on my damn walls in human shit," I finish explaining. "I *know* it was him, and now it looks like he may have done more than just vandalize my music room."

"What do you mean?" Grace asks sharply, her brow furrowing.

"Deputies found drugs and drug paraphernalia in my bedside table."

"Drugs? What kind of drugs?"

"Crystals. Meth, I think. I'm not sure."

I'm about to tell her about the bottle of scotch as well when Brant returns.

"Everything okay?" I ask him instead.

"Fine," he grumbles, and I wonder if he and Savvy had an argument over something.

∽

Brant

I'M DOING my best to get my frustration in check before I bite someone else's head off.

I about did that with my daughter.

Most of my frustration is with the Portland Police Department who apparently have a record of all of these wackos out there sending threats and bizarre stuff to Phil, but are still sitting on their goddamn hands now that someone has escalated to breaking into and defiling her house. Planting drugs. Shit, they may have even attempted to poison her.

Which is exactly what Savvy apparently told the detective she spoke to at the Portland PD after she'd found out about the bottle. She'd called them back and asked again for them to check on Duncan Brothers's whereabouts, but those guys still don't see it as a priority. I guess they're waiting for a damn body before it even pings on their radar.

Everybody's overstretched and understaffed. Even our own small sheriff's department is stretched thin, with Chief Deputy Alexander by his wife's bedside in Spokane, Deputy McCormick still at home recovering from surgery. Then this morning Jeff Sanchuk apparently called in sick, after Savvy gave him a piece of her mind when she caught him all but slapping handcuffs on Phil when he found drug paraphernalia in her nightstand.

Overzealous bastard. Always so quick to pull out the cuffs, eager to make the collar, but doesn't bother waiting for the evidence to come in. It's landed him in trouble more than a handful of times over the years, and has only gotten worse since Savvy took the office he'd been eyeing his entire career. Vindictive bastard too, calling in sick, knowing that means Savvy will likely have to work around the clock to try and make up for the slack.

So I'm pissed, because now I feel torn, wanting to give my daughter a hand before the workload takes her down, but I can't exactly leave Phil alone and exposed either.

"I'm going to put my stuff away," Phil's manager announces as she slips into the hallway to the guest rooms.

I guess she's going to be hanging around, which is almost complicating things.

Wrapping my fingers around Phil's wrist, I give her a little tug to the back door.

"Need to talk to you," I mumble by way of explanation when she raises her eyebrows at me.

Out on the deck, I steer her to the left, as far away from the guest rooms as we can get for privacy.

"Is something wrong?"

I hate seeing the worry in her eyes, so I force a smile on my lips as I use my thumb to unstick a stray curl caught at the corner of her mouth. Then I kiss her lightly.

"Logistical issues mostly," I share. "Savvy is short three deputies at this point, and in a department with only eight to begin with, it means overtime for everyone, including the sheriff, who already burns the candle at both ends."

"Can she hire someone?"

"Not easy. It's a struggle to get qualified people to join such a small force. Most of them prefer the big city where they'll see more action. And any qualified locals are already on the payroll. A few years back I started going into the schools in the county to do presentations. We now have one young deputy as a result of those talks, but it's a long-term investment with a small yield. We put out feelers in other departments and sometimes luck out when someone wants out of the rat race and to scale down their life, but still work in law enforcement. But we haven't had one of those since I hired Warner Burns three years ago."

"Could you help?" she asks, studying me closely.

I let my gaze drift to the river, where I'd love to be fishing with her again instead of worrying about her safety.

"I mean in the office," she clarifies. "Or even actively searching for new recruits," she adds with a smile.

"Once we have your situation under control, I will."

I can tell from her reaction she's not a fan of that answer.

"But wouldn't my *situation* get under control faster if the sheriff's department had some help?" she points out stubbornly.

I slide my hands around the side of her neck and bend down a little so we're eye to eye.

"Not if that means leaving you vulnerable," I explain.

I was half expecting anger, but not the burst of laughter exploding from her mouth. It immediately makes me want to kiss her again. How did I get infatuated with this woman so fast?

"Have you met Grace?" she asks, puzzling me. "She's been in charge of my security for almost twenty years. Besides, I'm sure she's armed. She usually is."

Armed? That piques my interest because, unless she has a valid concealed carry license for Washington or one that is recognized here, she would be breaking the law.

"Maybe I should have a chat with her," I announce, already moving to the back door.

"I'm pretty sure she's licensed," Phil calls after me, easily guessing the direction of my thoughts.

That I appear to be so transparent to her should concern

me, but instead it gives me a warm feeling inside. The deep level of understanding it conveys is something I've missed for a damn long time.

But it doesn't stop me from marching inside to have a word with her manager.

CHAPTER 13

B*rant*

WHO'D HAVE THOUGHT that thin rake of a woman was a police officer for the San Francisco PD many years ago?

She explained to me she did some moonlighting as security at a small concert venue, where she met Phil almost two decades ago. At the time, the band was about to embark on a worldwide tour, and they had a management company taking care of everything for all four band members, but being the only woman, Phil wanted someone who'd look out for her specifically.

I'd say that was a smart choice on Phil's part, and it apparently paid off for both, seeing as their working relationship survived the band's breakup.

Knowing the woman had successfully protected Phil for almost twenty years, and after Phil insisted, it was easier for me to hop in my Bronco and join Savvy at the sheriff's station.

"I'm surprised you're here," she comments when I walk into her office.

"Thought you might need a hand."

"What about Phil?" she asks pointedly.

"Looked after. Her manager is a former cop, did you know that?"

"She mentioned it when I spoke to her first thing this morning."

I take a seat across from her desk and notice she looks exhausted.

"So, what can I do? Put me to work."

She groans and presses the heels of her hands in her eyes.

"I can't even think straight anymore, Daddy. I feel like a squirrel on crack, running in twenty different directions, trying to keep up with the influx of information. So much is happening and I feel like I can't get ahead of it. I had a list of stuff to follow up on after yesterday I was going to get KC to help me with, and then this morning Sanchuk called in sick, so KC had to fill in for him on the regular rotation. And to top it off, we now have a poisoned goat, a possible attempted murder, and a moving box full of the most disturbing fan mail you can imagine to sort through."

She slides a file folder she has open in front of her out of the way, folds her arms on the desk and drops her head down.

I get a flash of Savvy as a teenager, overwhelmed or frustrated by some homework assignment, doing the exact same thing. I reach out and stroke her hair, like I used to do then.

"Have you eaten?" I ask gently.

"Not since breakfast," she grumbles.

"Can't think on an empty stomach, Toots," I remind her.

I grab the phone on her desk and dial one for reception, where Brenda Silvari, our office manager, answers right away.

"Sheriff?"

"It's Colter senior, Brenda. Could you order a large Hawaiian pizza and a Greek side salad from Pie Central?"

"Sure thing, Boss."

After twenty years working for me, I don't think Brenda will ever stop calling me that, so I don't even bother correcting her.

"And Brenda? If you plan on staying any longer, order yourself something and maybe add a couple of pies for the break room as well."

"Will do."

As soon as I hang up, Savvy lifts her head, looking at me through bleary eyes.

"You hate pineapple on pizza," she reminds me.

"I'll live. Now, what's next on your list?"

She slides the open folder across the desk at me. A handwritten note is on top. I quickly scan the items she jotted down before moving it aside. There is no particular rhyme or reason to her notes. Then I reach for the notepad on her desk and grab a pen from the collection of writing instruments tucked into an old coffee mug from the Bread and Butter diner that somehow ended up on her desk.

"Talk me through it," I urge her. "What do you know, what do you have, and what do you need?"

"Dad..." she groans. "We don't have time for this."

"Honey, if your mind is as scattered as your notes are, you're going to miss things. It'll help when you talk it through. Make time."

She sighs deep, but leans back in her chair and folds her

arms behind her head, letting her eyes drift out the window as she starts recounting events chronologically, while I take notes. When she's done, I look over the list I made and start asking questions.

"Fingerprints?"

"Yes, all over the instruments and furniture in the music room. We're still processing them and trying to eliminate people we know have had access, like Phil, her manager, the movers, her cleaning lady in Portland, and even the other band members. Those guys were over at her place in Portland before they did a charity concert last year."

"So, working from the theory it was this Duncan guy, if his fingerprints show up, they are easily explained," I point out.

"Correct. Except on the nightstand, the crack pipe, and the baggie which, by the way, held a combination of meth and fentanyl," she informs me. "Just like in Angus's stomach contents. Buck called me when I was on my way back to the office. I'm still waiting for a call from the lab on the whiskey and the blood samples we took from you and Phil."

"That's disturbing," I observe.

Meth laced with fentanyl is a lethal combination and the cause of many an unfortunate overdose. It's not difficult to see what the possible objective could have been here. There was a clear attempt to plant the seed Phil is an addict, so that a later overdose might have been ruled accidental. If I hadn't taken her home, things might have ended very differently. That tiny sip of whiskey we shared, before things got heated between us, could easily have been a full tumbler, maybe two, Phil would've had by herself in her own house.

"I know," Savvy confirms. "Anyway, back to fingerprints, we did find some on the bottle, but those belonged to Phil, you, and Grace, who helped Phil move in. Those are all accounted for. I don't think we'll find any that are useful to us, the lack of fingerprints on the crack pipe and baggie would indicate he was wearing gloves."

"Right. Next would be the biological material, but it'll take months before the lab can get DNA extracted."

"Besides, it may not even be his own shit," Savvy points out.

Disgusting.

"Gross. Moving on. Portland PD, any word yet?"

"No. I was going to call again in the morning."

"Ask for Assistant Chief Sondra Hollings, she runs the investigations unit. I've dealt with her before. She'll be able to light a fire under whoever you talked to before."

"I hope so."

"I know so," I assure her. "Okay, next question, how did he get in? You say there was no indication the alarm was actually turned off at any time?"

"No. And nothing visible on the exterior cameras either. I put a call in to Battaglia Security, spoke to Maggie, but she said Roy was on a job in Spokane and not answering his phone. She was going to tell him to call me. I haven't heard anything yet."

This is the way investigations sometimes go, it's a lot of waiting for others to provide the pieces so you can put your puzzle together. It can be frustrating, especially when you're not blessed with an abundance of patience, which Savvy has not. She takes after her father.

"All right. If you want, I can go chase down Roy," I offer. "Someone got in somehow, and knowing how that might've been done is gonna bring us closer to who would've been able to."

"After you eat," Brenda announces from the doorway, carrying a big pizza box and a brown paper bag.

I notice the shadows getting longer as the sun slips behind the peaks.

Dusk tends to be longer here in the mountains.

I wolfed down three slices of pizza, picking off as much of the pineapple as I could. Fruit does not belong on pizza, and even vegetables are questionable, if you ask me. Meat and cheese, what else do you need?

Steering my Bronco through the streets of Silence, my first stop is the Battaglia Security office, which looks closed. No lights on and no vehicles in the parking lot. Next I drive over to Mountain View, a more affluent neighborhood on the south side of town, where Roy and Maggie Battaglia live.

Roy's truck is here but I don't see Maggie's SUV when I walk up the driveway to the front door. It takes Roy a few minutes to get the door. His hair is still dripping from a recent shower.

"Sheriff, to what do I owe the honor?" he asks right away.

"Brant is fine, Roy. Savvy carries that title now."

He waves a hand at me. "I know, but old habits die hard. Come in."

He steps aside for me to pass. "Don't trip over the mess," he warns as I try to circumvent boots and tools and dirty clothes. "I walked in, stripped down where I stood, and beelined into a much-needed shower. Let me quickly tidy this up before Maggie comes home and has a fit. Go ahead and make yourself comfortable."

A few minutes later, he joins me in the living room.

"Can I get you a drink?"

"Appreciate it, but I'll pass. I'm actually helping Savvy

out. The office is shorthanded. I'm guessing Maggie didn't get a hold of you?"

He looks confused, confirming it.

"Maggie? No. I spent all day working in a crawlspace underneath one of the historic homes in the Lucas Place neighborhood in Spokane. Trying to install a state-of-the-art alarm system in a house that is nearly two-hundred years old is not an easy task. Why?"

He takes a seat on the armrest of a recliner across from me.

"You installed an alarm for Phyllis Woods. She bought the place from Savvy, just down the road from me."

He nods. "I did. Is something wrong? Did something happen?"

"At some point yesterday afternoon or evening, someone managed to get into the house and did it without setting off the alarm. But Phil set it when she left, and it was locked when she got home. Here's the kicker," I add, sitting forward and leaning my forearms on my knees. "The app on her phone shows no irregularities. No notifications the alarm was turned off at any time while she was gone. There is also nothing visible on the exterior cameras, other than Phil leaving and eventually returning."

"That's impossible," he states adamantly.

"Actually, I was with her, both when she left and when she returned home. Someone was definitely in her house, vandalized her music room among other things."

Roy looks at me slack-mouthed.

"Are you serious? I have no idea how that's possible. I installed that system myself." He holds up both his hands. "Every sensor on every door and window was installed with these hands. Heck, the woman's assistant or manager, or whatever she was, followed me around from room to room to make sure I didn't miss a thing."

I'm not a particularly technical person, but I know with the fast evolution of technology, whatever advantage is gained, is quickly followed by ways to undermine it.

"Is there a way to disable the alarm without it being visible on the app on her phone? Maybe if the power is cut off?"

He shakes his head. "It has a backup battery, and the moment the power went off, an alert would be sent to the alarm dispatch number and law enforcement, as well as whoever of my guys is on duty at the time would be sent to check it out."

I run a hand through my hair, even more stumped than I was coming here. I thought for sure there had to have been a way.

"As for the video feed," Roy continues. "From what I recall, we installed five mini cameras, mostly focused on the front and rear of the house, where most of the access points are. But...cameras can be avoided if you can find them or know where they are."

When I walk back to my vehicle five minutes later, I don't feel much wiser. But as I drive to the office, going over the information I got from Roy, a few things he said start niggling in the back of my mind.

I'm about a block away when a few pieces slide into place with a snap. I abruptly change direction and head up the mountain while calling Savvy.

I don't even give her a chance to speak.

"What if there wasn't just one, but two perps?"

CHAPTER 14

P*hil*

"Just leave that box over there."

I watch the cleaner leave the box of remnants of my Grammys and my gold and platinum albums in the corner of the garage where Grace told him to leave it.

It was Grace's idea to find someone able to come in right away to get the music room cleaned out. Even though someone had made an effort to get rid of most of the crap smeared on the wall and had attempted to air the room out, the smell of pot, urine, and human waste was still present, filtering all through the house.

I'm not sure how she managed to get a crew in on such short notice, but a woman and two men showed up a couple of hours ago. They worked like crazy, loading everything not salvageable onto the back of their truck, along with the carpet they ended up ripping out. There wasn't much that could be saved in terms of my instruments, but those can be replaced, as can the carpet. It's the awards, the things that carry more meaning, which are difficult to lose.

"I'll try to get replacements," Grace assures me when she catches my expression. "And if that's not an option, I'll find someone who can get those fixed."

I nod, giving the box one last look. Then I turn my gaze out the open garage doors to the cleaners who pile into their truck and drive off, the back loaded high with what's left of my belongings. With a sigh, I head back inside, leaving Grace to close the garage door.

Bleach fumes and some particularly pungent version of pine-scented cleaner assault my nose when I pass the stairs up to the loft. At least it doesn't smell like an outhouse in here anymore, I guess it's an improvement. Still, I move through my bathroom and bedroom to open the windows a crack, hoping the worst of the strong scents will have a chance to dissipate before I crawl into bed.

Bedtime will be sooner rather than later; I'm exhausted. The events of these past twenty-four hours or so have worn me plumb out, and in addition, I may still be feeling some of the effects of whatever was in that whiskey.

I quickly change into some clean comfort clothes—soft knit navy lounge pants and a matching oversized, long-sleeved shirt—and go in search of Grace.

Outside, dusk has settled in when I walk into the kitchen and find her sitting at the kitchen island, nursing a beer. Not a bad idea, but I need something in my stomach first, we kind of skipped dinner.

Diving into the fridge I pull out a beer, a wedge of brie, a piece of hard salami, and a cluster of grapes, putting all of it on the large bamboo board I keep on the counter. I grab a knife from the block and cut some chunks of cheese and sausage, and find a box of crackers in the pantry. Then I move the bamboo board to the island.

"Eat," I order Grace, who hasn't had anything to eat either, to my knowledge.

We dive into the simple, but satisfying, meal as we sip our beers.

"I meant to ask you," Grace breaks the comfortable silence after a few minutes. "Did you have a chance to stop into the bank? I'm gonna need the new account number."

Last time we spoke, I'd mentioned it would make more sense for me to open a bank account locally, so the money for the sale of the house could be transferred here, and I'd have easy access.

"With everything that's been going on, I haven't really had the time," I confess. "I'll get it done once this all settles down."

Which I hope it does soon. This is not how I imagined my life in Silence would be. Of course, neither was an affair with my neighbor, but I'm enjoying that unexpected perk to living here.

"I guess you didn't see the lawyer's email asking for the account number?"

"Haven't looked at emails at all. Not in a while."

My eyes dart to the living room where I keep my laptop, only to remember the sheriff still has it. Then I glance around for my phone, but I probably left that in the pants I just tossed in the hamper. I should probably fish it out and charge it before I go to bed.

At the thought of bed, I instantly yawn. I'm so tired.

"I can stop in at the bank tomorrow," I suggest, yawning again.

A quick glance at the clock shows it to be only a few minutes past nine, but I don't care, I need some rest.

"I'm sorry, I'm turning in early," I announce with an apologetic smile. "It's been an eventful few days."

Grace smiles back, waving off my apology. "By all means."

When I start cleaning up the crackers and cheese, she stops me.

"I'll take care of that. You get some rest."

"I should set the alarm," I point out.

"I've got that too," she assures me. "Go to bed."

"Give me a chance to close my windows first."

She gives me a thumbs-up.

Just before I duck into the hallway to my bedroom, I poke my head back into the kitchen.

"You're a lifesaver, Grace Pallatino, I know I don't tell you enough how much I appreciate you."

She seems startled and almost looks angry when she turns her eyes to me, but it's only a flash, an instant later she's cracking a smile.

"Whatever."

Walking down the hall, I can still catch a hint of that persistent pot smell the bleach hasn't been able to completely wash out. Still, I close the window in the bathroom, then brush my teeth and wash my face, before doing the same in the bedroom. I remember to grab my jeans from the hamper to check my pockets for the phone, but it's not there. I'll have to find it tomorrow, because I don't feel like looking tonight.

I turn on the small light on my nightstand, and flick off the overhead light. But when I move to the bed, something slams into my back with the force of a freight train, lifting me clear off my feet. I land face down on the bed, pressed down by a heavy weight on my back.

At first, I'm too shocked to react, but then I get a whiff of skunk the moment before an arm slips around my neck and a familiar voice whispers in my ear.

"I fucking warned you, didn't I?"

The sound of his voice sparks a rage inside me, triggering my fight response. I try to scream, but all I produce is a muffled, strangled whimper, before his hold on my throat tightens. I struggle against the force keeping my head and torso pinned to the mattress, but manage to get my knees under my body.

With every bit of strength I can muster, I buck my hips and try to roll us over. I only partially succeed, freeing one arm, but it's enough to scratch and claw at whatever part of him I can reach.

"Hold still, bitch," he hisses, trying to stay out of my reach.

The moment he shifts, I'm able to plant my foot in the mattress and heave him off me. I'm gasping for air so I can scream, as I try to get away from him, but he doesn't give up easily and grabs onto my ankle. Flipping on my back I have both hands free now and launch an attack on his face with one, gouging him with my nails, while I reach for the bedside lamp with the other.

No sooner have my fingers wrapped around the base, when a flash of steel has the blood freeze in my veins.

A rivulet of blood is running down from the corner of his eye where one of my nails found purchase. When he presses the tip of his blade in the hollow at the base of my neck and smiles, his teeth are stained red.

I don't even recognize the man anymore. His face is gaunt and sunken in, his eyes wild and almost vibrating in their sockets. He's tripping bad on something.

"What are you doing, Duncan?" I manage on a rasp, hoping to reach the friend he once was.

"Yeah, Duncan?" I suddenly hear Grace.

I shift my gaze to the doorway to find her standing there, a gun aimed at my attacker. Relief washes over me and I briefly close my eyes.

"Gracie?" He looks surprised.

"What are you doing?" she repeats my words, staring hard at Dunk.

He shakes his head, as if to clear it, but the knife remains at my throat.

"Taking care of business, Gracie"

"I don't understand," I interject, confused myself. "Call 911, Grace."

Her eyes fix on me and the moment I look into them I immediately know something is very wrong.

"I will, but not yet," she drawls lazily. "Not until Duncan here finishes the job. Finish the job, Duncan."

"But you said—"

"Not until you finish the job."

"What job? What is going on? What are you talking about?"

My voice reaches a panicked pitch as I try to wrap my head around what is happening.

Grace?

"I need my fix, Gracie," Duncan whines, the tip of the blade cutting my skin.

"And you'll get it, as soon as you fucking finish...the... job!"

Suddenly the blade disappears from my neck, but as I start rolling away, I get punched in the side. A sharp hot pain spreads, taking my breath as I involuntarily roll back. My eyes lock on Dunk, who looks like he's about to cry. I press a hand to my side, feeling something warm ooze between my fingers.

"Again," I hear Grace order and I shift my attention to her.

"Why? Why would you want to kill me?"

"Wait," Duncan interrupts. "You said hurt, not kill."

I catch the narrowing of Grace's eyes, before the shot goes off. A hot spray hits my face as the back of Dunk's head explodes. He collapses on the bed beside me.

"We were fine, you and I," she says calmly, as if she didn't just blow a man's brains out. "This would not have been necessary if you hadn't gotten a wild hair and bought a fucking house out in the middle of nowhere. I knew it was only a matter of time before it came to light."

"Know what?" I ask, my voice fading and my sight growing dim.

I'm desperate to understand, as Grace approaches the bed and reaches for the knife Duncan dropped, raising it over me.

But no answer is forthcoming and the last thing I hear is the loud reverberation of another gunshot before my world goes dark.

CHAPTER 15

B*rant*

ROY'S COMMENT someone had to have known the locations of the cameras stuck with me.

Grace immediately came to mind, especially since—according to Roy—she had seemed extremely interested when he was installing the alarm, but I don't think she was necessarily responsible for the damage to Phil's belongings.

For one thing, I noticed the suitcases she arrived with earlier bore luggage tags for this morning's flight from Portland. Also, the level of rage you'd expect with that kind of destruction would be hard to contain and seems unlikely for the controlled, buttoned-up woman.

There'd been something off about this from the start; the frenzied wreckage in the music room does not line up with the cold, deliberate way Phil was being set up to look like an addict. Almost like there were two different people involved. One who was enraged and unhinged, like Duncan Brothers was on that recording I heard of him, but the other would have to be cunning and manipulative.

It isn't that hard to imagine Grace as a calculating mastermind, using Phil's former bandmate as a weapon in some larger scheme.

"What do you mean? Two perps?" Savvy echoes.

My tires squeal as I take a corner too fast, and my heart is pounding in my chest.

"I don't think Brothers worked alone, there's no way he could've circumvented the alarm. Not without inside help."

Savvy doesn't respond immediately and I can almost hear her thinking.

"You think Grace—"

A loud car horn has me jerk on my steering wheel, narrowly avoiding a pickup with the right of way to the intersection I am blowing through. Luckily the road up the mountain is clear and I lean on the gas.

"Dad? What's happening? Where are you?"

She sounds like she's running, barking orders at someone.

"I left her with that woman, Savvy. I thought she'd be safe."

"Daddy, don't you do anything stupid. We're on our way."

But I'm already turning into Phil's driveway. Slamming the Bronco in park, I reach for the glove compartment where I keep my gun. I won't be going in unarmed this time.

"Honey, she means too much to me to wait around for the cavalry," I tell Savvy, before I end the call and tuck my phone in my pocket.

I approach the front door with some caution, well aware I wasn't exactly stealth in my approach. It's locked, but it looks like some lights are still on. When I peer in the dining room window, I can see light coming from the kitchen, but I don't see any movement.

A small surge of hope flares up perhaps I'm wrong, and Grace has nothing to do with this. They could be having a friendly drink on the back deck, or maybe they've gone to bed and simply left a few lights on. But my gut doesn't quite believe that.

So when I move left, to go around the house, I do it carefully. I pass the garage and poke my head around the corner. Halfway down, I notice faint light filtering from the small bathroom window and also from Phil's larger bedroom window, which is farther toward the back.

I take one step in that direction when I see a brief flash at the same time I hear the crack of a gunshot. My heart sinks, and for a moment I'm paralyzed with fear—for Phil—but then decades of experience kick in and I start moving.

Pressing my back against the siding, I approach the window, even as I hear vehicles coming up the driveway behind me. Then I take a deep breath in, and carefully poke my head around the frame. It takes my brain a second to process the scene inside; two on the bed—Phil is one of them—blood fucking everywhere, and Grace hovering over them, a gun in one hand and a large knife in the other.

No time to think.

I swing around, fully facing the window, and train my gun on the menacing figure. She doesn't even see me as I squeeze off a single shot.

Everything moves in slow motion, the impact of the bullet shattering the window before hitting the woman center mass, her body going down next to the bed. Unable to see her from my vantage point, I ignore the shards of glass sticking out of the frame, and climb through the window.

Everything in me wants to rush to Phil's side, hoping against all odds she is still alive, but I first have to make sure the threat is neutralized.

Leading with my gun, I round the bed to find Grace crumpled on the floor. She dropped her weapon but has the knife still clutched in her hand.

"I've got her, Dad," I hear my daughter's voice behind me.

I didn't even realize she was here.

I move aside so she can step around me and watch as she kicks the gun out of the way and swiftly removes the knife from the woman's hand. It's not until she kneels down beside her and checks her for a pulse I turn away.

Only then do I trust myself to look at the carnage on the bed. It's a man, a massive hole in the back of his head, suggesting the gunshot I heard was for him. At first glance it looks like Phil may have suffered a similar fate, her body almost as bloodied as the man next to her.

For a moment, I'm overwhelmed by the crippling pain of loss—as sharp and as gut-wrenching as I remember—and a wave of anger at the injustice of losing a woman I love twice in one lifetime, tearing an agonized howl from my gut, but then I catch movement. Nothing more than a slight rise of her chest, but it's enough to snap me into action.

CHAPTER 16

P*hil*

THE FIRST THING I see is a rumpled man, his big body curled up on a well-worn recliner in the corner of the room.

I recognize the hat covering his face.

The typical scent of hospital already alerted me to my whereabouts before I'd even opened my eyes. The dull heavy pain in my side and stomach registered next, triggering memories of what happened in my bedroom before I passed out.

I can only guess at what followed, although judging from the scrubs he's wearing, and the bandages covering his shoulder and arm, Brant got hurt in the process.

My mouth is parched and I turn my head, hoping someone may have left a cup of water on my nightstand. Looks like I'm in luck, but reaching it proves to be a bit of a challenge. Every little move results in big pain. I growl in frustration.

"You're awake."

Brant unfurls himself from the much-too-small chair, bleary-eyed and his hair sticking up all over the place. He appears to teeter a little as he gets to his feet, but manages to rush to the bed where he bends down to drop a sweet lingering kiss to my forehead.

"Hi," I croak, swallowing to try and get some saliva flowing. "What happened to you?"

"It's nothing," he tries to convince me. "Should I call a nurse? Can I get you something?"

"A sip of water, please."

He grabs the cup, feeds the straw between my lips, and I groan with relief when the still-cold water fills my mouth. When I've had my fill, he sets it down and pulls up a stool so he can sit beside me, clutching my hand.

"How are you feeling?"

"Sore, a bit groggy, and a lot confused," I confess.

He nods, as if it was no less than he expected.

"You're in the hospital. I'm not sure how much you remember, but you were stabbed and lost quite a bit of blood," he explains. "Apparently, the knife nicked an artery, so they had to open you up to stop the bleeding."

He points at the two bags hanging off an IV stand; one is clear liquid, and the smaller one is blood.

"They're working to get your blood levels back up."

The door opens and Savvy's friend, Dana, walks in, a smile on her face.

"Glad to see you awake. How are we doing?"

She immediately starts fiddling with a machine attached to the IV stand that started beeping.

"I'm okay. I'm here, so that's good."

"Yeah, I'd call that a win," she agrees. "You had us worried there for a bit. Didn't she, Sheriff?" she directs at Brant, who can't seem to take his eyes off me.

"Damn right," he mutters.

"He wouldn't leave your side. It wasn't until we wheeled you into the OR we were finally able to convince him to let us stitch him up."

I look at Brant, who aims a disgruntled glare at Dana, who doesn't seem impressed in the least.

"What happened?" I ask him, but it's Dana who ends up answering.

"Apparently climbed through a broken window to get to you, slicing himself up in the process."

I give his hand a squeeze to force him to look at me. When he does, I see the turmoil of emotions boiling in those blue eyes. I wonder what that scene must've looked like to him. Bile burns up from my stomach when I recall the moment Dunk was shot. The taste of his blood on my lips even as my own slipped through my fingers.

"I'm okay," I whisper for his ears only.

He nods once, swallowing hard.

"Use the button if you need anything, but for now I'll let you rest," Dana announces, "and I'll let Savvy know. I know she was waiting to hear."

I register her words but my focus is on Brant, who seems to be struggling with his emotions. I bring his hand, which has been clutching mine, to my lips and press a kiss on his knuckles.

"Talk to me," I urge him gently.

"Thought I'd lost you," he finally admits in a low voice, his head hanging down. "Figured getting lucky enough for love to find me twice in this life was too much to wish for."

"Oh, Brant..."

His eyes lift and lock on mine.

"I'm too cautious to be an impulsive man, but I'll be damned if I wasn't knocked clear on my ass when I met you. I know it's too soon, and I'm probably a sentimental fool for saying anything, but after last night proved once again how fleeting life can be, I'm not about to hold back. It is what it is."

After last night's nightmare—the horror I lived through, and the taste of bitter betrayal by friends still fresh in my mouth—Brant's words are like a beam of hope. I can actually see myself building a new life next to this man.

Narrowly escaping death has a way of putting things in very clear perspective.

"Too soon?" I respond. "Not for me. I'm forty-six years old and this is the first time I've had someone fall for just me, stripped down to basics. Sure, I've been blessed with an exciting life, have felt the adoration of many, but all of that was smoke and mirrors. People fell for the illusion. I've always known that, which is why I've never allowed myself the risk of falling in love. Until now."

I smile at him, watching the lines fan out from his eyes deepening, as he slowly cracks his own. A crazy moment of lightness after an otherwise traumatic experience for both of us. I have so many questions, so much is still unclear, but all that can wait. For right now I'm glad to be alive, glad to be sharing this brief pause in time with Brant.

Reality returns when Savvy breezes in the door minutes later, and the energy in the room instantly changes.

I notice Brant sits up straight as his daughter approaches, tension radiating off him.

∼

Brant

"Hey..." Savvy moves up to the bed and puts a hand on Phil's shoulder. "I'm so glad to see you awake. How are you doing?"

"I'm okay," I hear Phil's soft answer through the ringing in my ears.

The moment my daughter walked into the room, every nerve in my body went on alert.

Last night two ambulances were called. One for Phil, and one for Grace, who'd apparently been clinging on to life. I haven't wasted too much time thinking about Grace, since my entire focus has been on Phil.

Yet, suddenly I find myself wondering if she made it. Not because I particularly care about her, but because in the thirty years working in law enforcement, I'd never taken another person's life. I've discharged my gun, but never with a fatal outcome, and I'd rather not change that one year into my retirement. Not that I regret shooting her—I'd do it again in a heartbeat—but I'd just as soon not carry the responsibility for taking another life with me for the rest of mine.

That's why I'm suddenly on alert, trying to read my daughter's body language.

"Dad? Did you sleep at all?" she addresses me.

"Some."

She nods. "Do you guys feel up to answering a few questions? I want to get a few details straight for my report. I won't keep you long," she promises.

It feels weird sitting on this side of an interview for once. I'm pretty sure it's the shooting she's more concerned about at this point. I know she has to ask the hard questions, and it's especially important to make sure everything is done by the book since I'm her father.

"Of course," Phil tells her.

"Is she dead?" I want to know first.

Phil's hand twitches in mine, and I realize she may have blocked or missed a lot of what went on in that room. I regret being so blunt, but I need to know.

Savvy looks startled at my abrupt question at first, but then understanding floods her features.

"Geeze, Daddy, I'm sorry, I should've led with that. Too much on my mind. No, she ended up being airlifted to Spokane where she underwent surgery, but she's expected to live."

Relief has me deflate like a balloon, as all the tension I've been holding drains from my body.

"It'll be a while before I can question her though," Savvy continues. "Which is why it's important I get as much information as I can from you."

The last is addressed to Phil, who nods.

"Are you sure you're okay?" I ask her, noticing her wince.

She turns her eyes on me and produces a tired smile. "Yeah, let's get this done."

Rather than bombard Phil with questions, Savvy invites her to fill us in on the circumstances of last night. It's hard to listen to her recounting the events, especially when she explains how she was tackled to the bed by Brothers, who had already been in the house. She takes her time trying to recall what was said, but by the end of her account we have a pretty vivid picture of what happened.

"Maybe I'm still a little foggy," Phil states, "but it all still seems so surreal to me. I mean...why? I could tell Duncan was far gone, but I already knew that. He'd become a slave to the drugs and was a willing puppet to her, but what on earth could've motivated her? I've always treated her well. Hell, for the longest time she was the only friend I had. It's not like this was done in a flash of anger, she must've planned this for a while. But why?"

"All we can do is speculate, at this point," Savvy answers her. "But I think you're right, she used Duncan's anger to create a situation where all eyes would be on him. I think initially Grace hoped you'd overdose after drinking the whiskey. That would've been the ideal outcome for her, but when that failed, she had to come up with another plan. It sounds like she lured Brothers to your place with the promise of drugs, setting him up to kill you. She'd then shoot him, claiming self-defense. He was nothing but a weapon to her, set up to take the fall. But I don't think he wanted you dead. It's clear from what you told us he wasn't completely on board, so she was about to take matters into her own hands when Dad intervened."

"I'm willing to bet she somehow managed to sabotage your security system," I volunteer. "We should have Roy go over it with a fine-tooth comb."

Savvy grins at me. "Already on it." Then she turns back to Phil.

"As for motive, I may have an answer for you. We found your phone in your guestroom. We couldn't open it, but the screen showed several missed calls, and part of a text message from a Ken Winfield, marked urgent."

"That's my lawyer," Phil clarifies.

Savvy nods. "I know. I remembered seeing his name on the press release posted on social media debunking the overdose story. Anyway," she continues, "I contacted him to inform him of what happened, and he told me he'd been trying to get a hold of you. Apparently, something odd popped up when he was prepping the paperwork for the closing on the sale of the Portland property. When you first bought the house, you took out a line of credit on the property."

"I did. That was for renovations I wanted done to the place. I was still touring at the time, and Grace needed a way to pay contractors." She shakes her head. "But I paid that outstanding balance when I finally got home and closed that account."

"I'm guessing Grace was supposed to take care of that?" I suggest.

"That was for half a million dollars," she shares, looking shocked.

"Actually, make that one million and then some," Savvy fills her in. "The account was never closed, and the money you paid into it is gone too. According to Ken, this is just the tip of the iceberg. He's uncovering more stuff."

As realization sets in, I watch Phil's energy drain, leaving her looking sunken and pale.

"Good God," she mumbles, her eyes closing.

"That's enough for now. She needs rest," I tell my daughter.

"Of course. What about you, Daddy? You should go home and get some rest too."

"You should," Phil agrees, barely able to lift her eyelids.

"I'm not going anywhere."

Savvy rolls her eyes at me and grumbles, "Stubborn old coot."

That draws a snort from Phil.

"Stubborn, I can see. But I'm not so sure about the *old* part. From what I've seen of him, he's still in prime working order."

Savvy slaps her hands over her ears.

"Don't tell me that. It's bad enough I had to hear from

Auden Maynard you two were getting it on in the parking lot by Bear Lake."

Groaning, I drop my head down on the edge of the mattress, while Phil softly chuckles.

I knew that was going to come back to haunt me.

CHAPTER 17

P*hil*

"Let me do the work."

He stretches my arms over my head and, with one hand circling my wrists, holds them in place. With his other hand he hooks me behind the knee, spreading me wide open. Then he begins to move again, more slowly than the pace I was trying to force in my rush toward the orgasm he's been keeping me from.

This is a game he plays; working me into a blind frenzy to where I can barely take another breath, before slowing down the pace and leaving me aching. He plays it so well, I'm almost ready to throttle him, even though I already know the end result will have me seeing stars.

His heavy breath is in my hair, his strong body curved over me, and his thick cock filling me with every careful stroke.

"Please, Brant, harder. I'm so close."

"I know," he whispers, not moving any faster.

In my frustration, I sink my teeth into the tendon at the base of his neck. He groans deeply, the sound vibrating through my body, and then his control finally snaps. His hips piston as he powers inside me, grunting with the effort, and I find myself rushing to the apex.

When my body finally flies apart, every synapse in my body firing off signals like Fourth of July fireworks, my heart stops, and I momentarily forget how to breathe. All I can do is cling on for dear life, riding out the force that is Brant, until he too flies off the edge, before collapsing on top of me. When he lets go of my wrists, I fold my arms around him, holding him right where he is.

My mind drifts as we each try to catch our breath.

It's been over a month since I was attacked in my own home, and this is the first time I've spent the night back in my room. I've been staying at Brant's place, and he would've happily kept me there, but I'm not ready to give up the house I fell in love with to bad memories.

I'm determined to reclaim this place as my own.

I'm glad Brant stayed over, but I would've spent some time here either way. It's not that I don't want him in my space—he's more than welcome here—but I want a home that feels like my own. Brant's house is great, but there's a lot of history there I'm not a part of. Here I feel confident of my place in the world.

Even if it means going back and forth between houses for now, I don't mind. Why not? If that's what works for us.

The bed is new, obviously, as is the window, and Brant went ahead and repainted the room in a soft sage I really love. The music room upstairs has been given a facelift as well, with a nice, new cork floor that is supposed to absorb sound, and freshly painted walls as well. I already bought a new keyboard, and plan to replace some of the other instruments that were lost.

Last night, before we went to bed, Grant took me up there to show me what he and Buck had been working on in his barn a few nights this past week. My two Grammys were on full display on a floating shelf he installed on my wall. The awards had been painstakingly soldered back together and seeing them restored brought tears to my eyes. The gold and platinum records they had pieced together as best they could, and those were attached to a live-edge plank of wood, which was hung underneath the floating shelf.

It makes for a great focal wall I can start rebuilding my music room around.

Brant knows nothing of music, other than what he enjoys listening to, but he's showing me he understands its importance in my life, and I couldn't be more grateful for that.

For *him*.

He grunts against my shoulder and presses a kiss to my skin.

"Shower?" he asks, as he untangles himself from me.

I'm sticky and sweaty, so my answer is immediate. "Definitely."

Half an hour later, we are sitting out on the deck, stretched out on my awesome lounge chairs, having a coffee and a bagel, when the doorbell rings at the front of the house. Before I can even put my coffee down, Brant is already on his feet.

"I've got it."

My eyes follow him, but with the sun reflecting off the glass door, I can't track him inside. So I turn back to face the creek, rest my back against the chair, and enjoy the view until I hear the door open.

"He says he'll take him back if you've changed your mind."

Unsure what he's talking about or even who he's talking to, I sit back up and swing around. My face cracks open with a wide smile when I see who he brought out here.

"Oh my goodness, Diesel!"

At the sound of his name, the dog rushes toward me, his entire back end wagging.

I hadn't mentioned the dog; at first, because I was still recovering and didn't want to burden Brant—who was already looking after me—to take on another dependent, and later because I was afraid to find out he'd already found another home.

I throw my arms around the dog and smile at Brant over Diesel's big head.

"Not a chance in hell I'm changing my mind."

He grins back. "Didn't think so."

"I was afraid he'd found another home," I confess.

"Buck held on to him. Fattened him up some. I was kinda waiting for you to bring him up, but when you said you wanted to start spending time at your house again, I figured the time was right."

"You figured correctly," I inform him, letting go of the dog and getting to my feet.

I watch as Diesel wanders off toward the creek for a drink.

"Do I have to worry about him taking off?" I ask Brant, who approaches and drops his arm around my shoulders, pulling me to his side.

"Nah, Buck says he spent some time training him and his recall is pretty good."

I turn in his arms and place my hands on his chest, looking up into his clear blue eyes.

"What did I do to deserve you?"

His arms tighten around me.

"Should be me asking that question."

I shake my head. "I've done nothing. You're the one who's been looking after me," I remind him.

"Nothing?" he reacts. "Phil, don't you know I wake up every morning looking forward to the day ahead because of you?"

I'm not a sentimental person, I tend to show emotion through my music, but the beautiful simplicity of his words strikes a chord, and I find myself blinking at tears.

"God, I love you."

The lines by his eyes crinkle as his smile deepens.

"Right back atcha, Sweetheart."

~

BRANT

I FEEL BETTER LEAVING her to putter around her house, knowing she has the dog looking out for her and the alarm is working as it should.

That bitch, Grace, had disabled the alarm on the window in the garage. Apparently, the alarm goes off when a magnetic relay is broken as a window opens. She mounted a powerful magnet right underneath the contact on the window sill, which ensured the relay remained intact, even with the window open. No alarm would sound, and since the connection remained uninterrupted, no notification would show up.

It had been Duncan Brothers's way in.

Grace survived the bullet in her stomach, but she's currently sitting in jail, and is likely to spend the rest of her life there. It's where she belongs. Savvy mentioned Grace lawyered up right away, but they won't need a confession, there appears to be more than enough evidence to ensure a conviction without it.

With the help of Phil's lawyer, my daughter was able to put together a compelling picture, illustrating the scope of Grace's deceit. She had been stealing money from Phil for years, living well above her means. Greed and jealousy motivated her, and fear of discovery ultimately propelled her into violence.

I'm on my way into town, at Phil's urging.

Earlier today she clued in to the fact I haven't been to any of our Thursday poker nights since she was attacked, and insisted I join my friends for tonight's game. When I invited her to come, she laughed and told me I wouldn't want her there unless I was ready to lose my shirt. It's a challenge I'd love to take her up on at some point, but for tonight she wanted to stay home and catch up on some TV baking show. I can't say I'm sad to miss that, although I've become a big fan of some of Phil's kitchen creations. A little too big, maybe; my jeans are getting tight.

"The prodigal son returns," Clem calls out when I walk into The Kerrigan.

"Finally, he comes up for air," Keith Jespers—back from his cruise—adds his jab.

"Have you *seen* the woman he's shacked up with?" Buck, of course, has to put his two cents' worth in.

All three of them are hanging at the bar with Jacob.

"Yeah, yeah, yeah."

I wave them off, but I do it grinning.

"Is that a smile, or gas?" Jacob decides to join the fun at my expense.

"Leave the man alone, Dad," Dana, who appears to be slinging beers tonight, scolds her father.

Ignoring the men, I focus on Dana.

"How come you're working tonight?"

"Mom's in Coeur d'Alene visiting her sister," she shares before asking, "Can I get you a drink?"

"Unsweetened ice tea would be good."

"Coming right up."

When she hands me my drink, I thank her and follow the guys into the back room.

"For all the ribbing..." Jacob starts when he takes the seat beside me, clapping me on the shoulder. "Glad for you, my friend."

I nod in his direction, a bit uneasy with the attention.

"Hear, hear," Buck cheers, lifting his glass. "You're a lucky bastard, Brant. You hit the jackpot."

"I know it," I confirm.

"You should've brought her," Clem suggests, as he shuffles a new deck of cards. "Maybe she'd like to sit in for a couple of hands."

"If she doesn't know how to play, I'm more than happy to teach her," Buck offers magnanimously.

Now that would be something to look forward to; bringing Phil in as a ringer. I'd enjoy watching her wipe the floor with these guys.

But either way, I look forward to introducing her to the rest of Silence.

"I'll see if she can make it next week."

I can barely keep the grin off my face.

ALSO BY FREYA BARKER

HMT 2G:

HIGH FREQUENCY

HIGH INTENSITY

HIGH DENSITY

HIGH VELOCITY (2025)

High Mountain Trackers:

HIGH MEADOW

HIGH STAKES

HIGH GROUND

HIGH IMPACT

Arrow's Edge MC Series:

EDGE OF REASON

EDGE OF DARKNESS

EDGE OF TOMORROW

EDGE OF FEAR

EDGE OF REALITY

EDGE OF TRUST

EDGE OF NOWHERE

GEM Series:

OPAL

PEARL

ONYX

PASS Series:

HIT & RUN

LIFE & LIMB

LOCK & LOAD

LOST & FOUND

On Call Series:

BURNING FOR AUTUMN

COVERING OLLIE

TRACKING TAHLULA

ABSOLVING BLUE

REVEALING ANNIE

DISSECTING MEREDITH

WATCHING TRIN

IGNITING VIC

CAPTIVATING ANIKA

Rock Point Series:

KEEPING 6

CABIN 12

HWY 550

10-CODE

Northern Lights Collection:

A CHANGE OF TIDE

A CHANGE OF VIEW

A CHANGE OF PACE

SnapShot Series:

SHUTTER SPEED

FREEZE FRAME

IDEAL IMAGE

Portland, ME, Series:

FROM DUST

CRUEL WATER

THROUGH FIRE

STILL AIR

LuLLaY (a Christmas novella)

Cedar Tree Series:

SLIM TO NONE

HUNDRED TO ONE

AGAINST ME

CLEAN LINES

UPPER HAND

LIKE ARROWS

HEAD START

Standalones:

WHEN HOPE ENDS

VICTIM OF CIRCUMSTANCE

BONUS KISSES

SECONDS

SNOWBOUND

ABOUT THE AUTHOR

USA Today bestselling author Freya Barker loves writing about ordinary people with extraordinary stories. With 60+ titles to her name, Freya inspires with her stories about 'real' people, perhaps less than perfect, each struggling to find their own slice of happy.

Freya has her hands full with a retired husband, a needy pup, and a growing gaggle of grandbabies, but she continues to spin story after story with an endless supply of bruised and dented characters, vying for attention!

Recipient of the ReadFREE.ly 2019 Best Book We've Read All Year Award for "Covering Ollie, the 2015 RomCon "Reader's Choice" Award for Best First Book, "Slim To None", Finalist for the 2017 Kindle Book Award with "From Dust", and Finalist for the 2020 Kindle Book Award with "When Hope Ends", Freya spins story after story with an endless supply of bruised and dented characters, vying for attention!

www.freyabarker.com